KINGDOM OF STORMS

THE DESERT CURSED SERIES, BOOK 8

SHANNON MAYER

HiJINKS

ACKNOWLEDGMENTS

Sometimes a book takes more time than you think it will need. This was one of those books. Not because of Zam, Maks and Lila, but because of real life. 2021 has been a year of trials for me, and the exhaustion finally caught up to my brain and . . .well . . .things were tough.

But I found my footing again, and the book flowed, and my brain finally let me write. Thank you for your patience, and for you understanding. Thank you for your support. Thank you for being my people.

And for those who don't want to be patient or understanding . . .I'll await your scathing emails and be sure to share them with Satan—I mean my author friends—over a cup of tea as we decide how to respond. :)

1

"Now is the winter of our discontent," Lila muttered under her breath, right in my left ear. I didn't look over at the pint-sized dragon, but I did reach up and tug at her tail. She dug her talons into my shoulder to keep her balance, then whapped me with one of her wings.

"Don't egg karma on, we don't need fate to choose today to shit on us," I said, brushing her wing away from my face.

We had not had a good go of things. Sure, we'd found the Vessel of Vahab—the first challenge facing us on our way to deal with the Beast from the East. Sure, we'd saved the unicorn herd. But we'd lost Torin —Balder's father. Maks was stuck with some psycho who wanted him to father her a child. And we were here, in the middle of fucking nowhere in the middle of this fucking storm.

Running from Asag instead of facing him.

The desert night wind blew sharp and deadly cold in a way I wasn't sure I'd ever felt in any section of our western desert, spinning my words away from my mouth. This far south and east the sands should never have felt anything more than a warm rain. Even a flood could happen on a regular basis, but nothing *this cold*. Nothing that felt like we were in the far northern climes.

Yet here we were riding head on into a storm that screamed magic, witchery, and just a general 'someone doesn't like you, so have fun with this while they try to kill you' kind of vibe. I mean, come on. *Icicles* dangled from Balder's mane and off bits of my saddle, even my own hair. The sand crunched under his hooves, and under the mare's hooves next to us.

Lila shivered where she was but didn't leave my shoulder. The cold was only part of the danger. She knew as well as I did that more could come on us in a flash.

Even with the cold, Balder had his head down as he kept on moving straight into the wind, trooper that he was—he was no slouch when it came to shitty weather.

A quick glance at my other side showed me the other horse, Dancer, tucked tight to Balder's hip, her face close to my knee. Her petite rider was wrapped in her cloak and hunched over the saddle to keep the wind out of her face, hands tucked close to her body.

She didn't need to have her hands on the reins; Dancer would follow Balder anywhere.

I reached back and put a hand on Reyhan's shoulder. She wasn't shivering, at least, so that was good—shifters tended to run hot and that would help her here. Reyhan couldn't have been more than five or six years old. But like so many shifters, she was mature for her age in both her mind and her ability to survive. She'd faced the vampire-like rabisu alongside me, the winged rhuk, and she'd seen me take on the Nasnas monster and the oversized crocodile beasts.

I squeezed her shoulder gently and she lifted her head and smiled at me before tucking herself back under her cloak. If I could have left her behind at Mamitu's home I would have, because I had no doubt that there would be more monsters ahead of us and taking a child on a journey like this was not a great idea.

Why didn't I leave her behind? Asag, the Beast from the East, was on the move, headed straight to Mamitu's to punish her, all because I'd passed the first test that would allow me into his realm, the realm of demons. A test that *he'd* set out—yeah, it made very little sense to me too. Worse and worse, Asag had a thing for young shifter girls. Of which Reyhan was, and I was not about to let her get taken by a demon.

For that alone, I was looking forward to killing him, even if he hadn't been stealing away the dragon hatchlings for years. The blade strapped to my back whispered inside my head. *I look forward to the demon's death as well. I will help you. We will destroy him together.*

I grit my teeth, and struggled to keep my hands on the saddle, as I whispered under my breath. "Shut up, Lilith."

Lila swung around so she hung from the front of my neck and looked up into my face, tiny bits of frost clinging to the tips of her wings making them an even darker blue-purple. "Are you okay? She talking to you?"

"Lilith is . . . encouraging me to be violent," I said and shifted my shoulders as if that would settle the weapon's murderous words. That pull of her magic was stronger than I wanted to let on.

I'd dealt with a sentient weapon before, I could deal with Lilith too. I just had to get used to her.

Lila's ridged brows furrowed, and she crawled back up to my shoulder. "Maybe don't pick a cursed weapon next time, how about that? How about just a nice, normal killing tool. Not one that wants to kill you. Not one that wants to help you kill. Just . . . a normal weapon. One that doesn't talk."

I snorted. "Yeah, I'll keep that in mind." Not that I'd had a ton of choice. I'd felt the pull to Lilith from the second I'd stepped into the armory at Mamitu's, and I'd known that for whatever reason, I'd needed to take her with me. It. Damn it, I did not need this right now. I shoved all the pull of the weapon down deep, blocking out her mutterings as best I could.

Because right now . . . now we were riding deep into

the night to put as much distance between us and Mamitu's as we could before we stopped, and even though the fatigue was tugging on me, I felt that urge to keep going. Asag was behind us, and his eyes would turn our way in no time.

Sure, he'd laid out three tasks that had to be completed before anyone faced him, but I had no doubt that he would do everything in his power to stop me along the way.

A particularly hard, cold gust of wind slapped us in the face, stealing my breath.

"How much further are you going to push this?" Lila asked through chattering teeth. "You know that even Balder will have to rest at some point, and Reyhan is about ready to fall out of the saddle."

I sighed and looked over at the young girl bobbling in the saddle, clutching at it with her tiny hands. "You're right."

"Of course I'm right. I'm a dragon."

My face was cold enough that smiling was not an option, my skin tight, partially frozen.

"Reyhan," I called out over the wind. "I need you to shift."

She turned her head, big green eyes wide for a moment, and then she blinked and was a tiny jungle cat cub balanced on the middle of the saddle. I held a hand to her, and she leapt up to me. I tucked her under my cloak, and she started purring as my body heat sunk into her.

"Balder. Let's find some shelter, my friend. We all need a break." I urged him into a quick trot which brought the wind smacking into my face. I didn't dare go any faster, and not just for the cold. In the dark on uneven icy ground, a full out gallop was reserved for emergencies only. We did not need a broken leg. Not when there was no one who could heal it.

I clamped down on my thoughts of emergencies lest the fates decide even that was tempting them.

The sky above us was deep with thick clouds so there was no light even from the stars, but between my shifter abilities and Balder's keen eyes we made our way down a slope onto a flat plain that was surrounded on all sides by high cliffs. "There. On the other side."

I pointed at the stepped walls on the northern side, a good mile away. Even at that distance I could see that there were large dark patches in the sandstone walls.

Caves.

As I pointed, the first blotch of solid frozen rain hit my face with a gust of wind, stinging like a bite. One, and then more, and more. The deep clouds opened and let loose a barrage of hail.

"Let's go, quick as we can!" I yelled over the suddenly flying icicle pieces. I tugged my cloak over my face as best I could. At least Reyhan was out of this. Lila slid down the back of my cloak and tucked herself out of the weather.

Balder grunted and Dancer squealed as they were pelted all over their exposed hides.

Lila hid inside the back of my hood. "Ouch! This is the shits!"

The horses raced across the open, flat valley. We galloped the distance to the far side in less than a minute, but even that little bit of time cost us. My cheek was slashed open, and my hands were pelted as I clung to the reins. Flecks of blood flew back from the wounds blitzing open on the horses with each chunk of hail. So sharp, more like little daggers than rounded hail . . . far beyond what it should be, which lent itself to my belief that this was no natural storm.

A sensation buzzed over my skin of a magic that felt . . . like my own. Impossible? I turned my head toward the sensation to look up into the sky.

Eyes stared back at me from the clouds, and in a flash of lightning they were gone. But I'd seen them.

The question was who the hell was trying to kill us now? Asag? Somehow, I didn't think so.

In a split second, we were out of the storm. Balder slid to a stop just inside one of the caves, and I leapt off his back, clinging to Reyhan and staring out into the darkness. One last chunk of sharp hail shot at me and smacked the back of my head, making me stumble.

Even with that, I hesitated to go further into the cave that we'd been forced to take shelter in.

I'd survived this long in my life for a reason.

There was no way to know what waited inside the cave—another creature, another traveller, a big ass monster who hadn't eaten for three months.

But we couldn't stay out here, and I made the decision quickly as more hail slammed into and around us.

"Get in, get in!" I waved at the two horses, and they trotted into the cave, their bodies covered in miniature slices, skin flecked with blood and twitching as if that would rid them of the wounds.

I followed, pausing at the entrance next to Balder's hip.

Not so long ago I'd faced a creature, a rabisu, that couldn't cross the threshold of a doorway without an invitation.

There was a sudden flash of lightning, and I stared out across the open space we'd just galloped. There was nothing on the ground following us.

But movement in the sky drew my eyes upward. Sinuous and long, like a serpent. Was that attached to the eyes I'd seen?

Another flash of lightning and I was sure there was something flying above our heads.

I stepped further into the cave, cradling Reyhan with one arm. "Lila, do not fly out there, but can you see what it is?" I pointed to the wrath-filled sky.

She crawled up to my shoulder and peered out with me, eyes straining against the dark and the storming weather. "Nothing, I got nothing."

There were no more flashes of lightning and the ice rain continued to fall in larger and larger chunks. Ice rocks pounded down to the ground with enough force that I wasn't convinced someone hadn't hired giants to throw them at us.

Again, that made me think that the eyes had been looking for or at us, and literally taking shots.

Even so, knowing that, I stood my ground at the entrance. What if Asag had one of his captive dragons following us? That was my first thought with the flying creature. The second was that we'd taken up hiding in a creature's cave and he or she would show back up when we least expected.

"Whatever it is," Lila said, "I don't see it now. What do we do? You think it lives here, whatever it was?" Her question echoed my own. But with the hail, there was no choice. We couldn't survive out there. If we'd taken longer to leave Mamitu's, we wouldn't have made it. Being caught out in the open desert, there was no way we wouldn't have been pummeled to death.

"Keep going," I said, bumping into Balder's rump, pushing him further into the darkness, away from the entrance.

The shattering of a boulder-sized chunk of ice speared through the doorway and into the cave, scattering across our feet. If we'd been even a few feet closer that would have been a problem.

Again, that sensation buzzed along my skin of a magic that felt . . . like my own. A female Jinn maybe?

I shook my head. Who had I pissed off lately that was a woman?

My jaw dropped as the answer hit me as surely as one of the hailstones would have.

"What do you want to bet that's the Storm Queen?" I muttered as we worked our way deep enough into the cave that we could see the opening but weren't getting slashed or speared by the shrapnel of the ice explosions. "She has Maks. She controls the weather and we killed one of her rhuk."

Lila groaned. "Hell hath no fury like a woman scorned. You think that Maks turned her down?"

"I'm sure of it," I whispered.

"Then she's trying to kill you?" Lila nodded. "That makes a wicked sort of sense." She flew around my head as we went deeper into the cave. "I would like to ask the Toad if he thought that his idea was a good one. You know, getting caught by a woman who has the ability to wreak havoc on the weather. Why couldn't it just be a lonely old lady in the desert with a crush on him? One that would make him muffins every week. And call him sweety-buns. No, he had to go and make frenemies with—by all accounts—a psycho."

I sighed and went to my knees, without even the energy to laugh. Because Lila was right, this was a terrible situation—though she was wrong, it was no choice that Maks had made. Maks being caught by the Storm Queen had changed everything. Instead of working our way through the three challenges, to face Asag and free the dragon hatchlings, now we had to deal with the Storm Queen and save Maks. We had to save my mate. There was no other option in my mind.

Because with him at my side, I could face anything —even a demon.

Balder dropped his nose and worked his tactile lips across my cheek.

I lifted my hand and held his warm nose to my face, whiskers tickling my cheek. "Thanks, friend."

He blew out a long snort and lay down next to me. Starting a fire wasn't going to happen, so I leaned against the curve of his neck and shoulder and just closed my eyes.

I wasn't sleeping.

I just needed . . . a moment. The last twenty-four hours had been . . . well, rough was an understatement. We'd lost Torin, Balder's father. We'd escaped the rhuk and managed to get to Mamitu's. I'd faced down Vahab, and now we were on the run again. Not to mention the whole Maks being caught up by the Storm Queen who wanted to make cubs with him.

My guts clenched at the thought of the Storm Queen having her way with my mate. Jaw ticking, I struggled to breathe normally, to bring my heart rate into some semblance of normal.

We still had to get through the mountains to Pazuzu, the next guardian that Asag had in place to keep his realm safe. Somewhere in all that were the dragon hatchlings that needed rescuing.

But first, Maks.

A slow hiss of breath escaped me.

Reyhan shuffled in the crook of my arm, getting herself more comfortable or maybe just protesting that I was holding her a little tighter as I struggled and waded through some heavy emotions.

There was one other person, though, that I'd been decidedly ignoring for the last eight or so hours.

The person who had some seriously big mojo by all accounts and who had at one point really pissed people off. I mean, they'd stuck him an oversized flower vase.

Against my hip, the Vessel of Vahab shook and shivered. Opening my eyes, I fumbled with my free hand to press it against the top of the vessel. It really did look a bit like a flower vase with a lid. Bronze, etched with only a single symbol on it and it held the very first Jinn ever. Vahab. Demon-created. Which meant, well, it meant that there was some demon in me too if this was real. Bile rose in my throat.

Nope, I didn't like that much. I was part Jinn, and if all Jinn were from Vahab . . . ugh. I did not like that reality, but it was at the moment the easier thing to think about, rather than thinking about Maks naked with another woman and knocking her up.

Vahab's voice echoed out of the container. "We are at rest; I can feel no movement. Open this container so we can discuss my release."

I snorted and pushed my concerns away. "We can discuss it right now, while you are still in there. Otherwise, I've released you, and then we are discussing your release? That makes no sense." For good measure I knocked on the vessel with a closed fist.

The bronze container rattled as if he'd kicked it. In my mind I could see him throwing a tantrum like an oversized toddler and that made me smile. Sure, he was the first Jinn, and I really should have been more afraid, but he was stuck in a bottle. Jinny in a bottle as it were.

"You promised!" he roared, and the sound echoed through the cave. I looked back toward the entrance and the still crashing ice balls as they slammed into the desert out there. How long would the Storm Queen rage? Hopefully she'd run out of juice by morning.

"I promised to discuss your release. I did not promise you I would let you out again," I pointed out. Because I was no fool, I knew how a power like him could be if I wasn't careful. Manipulative and dangerous to not only me, but to those I loved.

I kept a hand on the container. "Let us be honest with one another, Vahab. And perhaps I will consider letting you out."

That stilled the bronze vessel under my hand. "How will I know you are honest, and how will you know I am honest?"

A good question.

Bind your words on my edge, Lilith whispered. *And your honesty will be assured.*

I frowned. "Lilith says—"

"LILITH?" If I thought his voice was loud before, it

was nothing to the roar that blasted out of him. "WHERE IS SHE?"

The bronze container almost vibrated out from under my hand. I sighed. "I should have known. Let me guess, you have a history with her too?"

"She is a terrible, terrible beast of a woman!" Vahab spit out, his voice echoing now only inside the container. "And I *hate* her. She is . . . arg, perhaps I will stay inside here after all."

"If we bind our words on her edge, she says that will keep us honest," I said. "Sound like a deal?"

He was quiet, the vessel still for a long time. Long enough that I thought perhaps he'd rather not speak to me ever again and stay within his container rather than deal with Lilith. Which was more than a little unnerving considering the fact that I was carrying her openly as my current weapon of choice.

"What do you mean, bind on her edge?"

I closed my eyes. "She is trapped inside a weapon."

He started to laugh and then that laugh turned into the braying of a man who could not control himself. A heaving gasp was his final noise before he spoke again. "She got herself trapped too? Serves her right!"

I rolled my eyes. "She is my weapon now. Do you want to bind your words by her blade or not?"

"She will kill us both given the chance," he grumbled.

I rolled my eyes. "Now tell me something I don't know."

His sigh was heavy as they come. "She is, perhaps *was* is the better word, my ex-wife."

Well now. . . *that* was not what I'd expected to come out of his mouth.

"And she's been trying to kill me for a very long time," he added.

I grinned. "I wish I could have introduced you to Steve."

The container rumbled. "Who is that?"

"My ex-husband," I said. "And I killed him once, brought him back from the dead, and killed him a second time. Just for fun." Okay, so that was a little bit of an exaggeration, but it got the point across.

A muttered curse rolled from the container and Lilith laughed softly in my head.

I knew there was a reason I liked you so, desert girl.

2

Bonding with a psychotic weapon over the double-death of my ex-husband was not really how I'd seen my day ending up.

But here we were. Doing just that in a cave in the middle of the desert while we waited out a deadly storm. Lilith's voice cooed to me. *I look forward to killing with you. If you would kill your own ex-husband, perhaps you will help me kill mine as well.*

I shook off the sensation urging me to grab hold of the short sword and go to town on a bloody killing spree aimed at the vessel at my feet.

Instead, I shifted my seat so that I leaned against the wall of the cave that we were hiding in and forced my breathing and energy to calm. The weather outside was not slowing down in its efforts to kill us so we were going to be here at least until morning. The wind whipped into a frenzy that lifted some of the melon-sized ice balls that had already fallen and flung them deeper into the cave, closer to us. The crashing and shattering of ice exploded, echoing into the cave, shards coming dangerously close even this far in. Could the Storm Queen have known that we were here? Or was she just throwing her weight around, knowing that if we were in the open, she had us dead to rights?

My bet was on the second thought, but just in case . . ..

"Back up." I stood and pushed the two horses ahead of me. Reyhan didn't so much as wiggle in my arms and Lila stayed tight to my shoulder.

The cave curved to the left and dropped down a few feet, hiding us completely from view of the outside world. The back wall was rounded—we'd gone as far as we could down the tunnel. Here's hoping it was far enough.

I dug through my saddlebag and pulled out an old flashlight that I'd turned into a proper torch on our trek south. With my flint and steel, I lit the top and gave the leather-wrapped torch to Lila.

"Hold this for me." I handed the torch to her. She scooped it, fluttered to the floor and sat on her round bottom, whipping her tail back and forth in the loose dust.

"I wish I could blow fire," she said.

"Your acid is plenty badass," I reminded her.

"But fire would be handy all the time. The acid is

only good once in a while." She put her claw tips into the flame one at a time.

Scouring the back of the cave, I found a few chunks of old wood, some brush and bits and bobs that would act as fuel for a fire. A few minutes later I had a good flame going and set about stripping the horses of their tack so they could rest easier.

Rules of the desert were simple, and rest while you could, that was one of the most important ones. Because if you had nothing in your reserves, you would die.

Saddles and bridles off, I fed the horses oatballs, went back out to the mouth of the cave and scooped up some ice to melt it for water for them. Only then did I let myself sit and breathe.

My peace lasted for about 2.3 seconds.

"I want out." Vahab rattled the vessel he was in. "Now. If Lilith is bound up, then I will be sure to avoid her."

I rolled my eyes. As if he had room to demand anything locked in a vase. "Listen, I can't trust you. So, unless you want to swear on Lilith's blade—"

"You can't trust Lilith," he snapped. "She would kill me and your friends if given the chance, just to prove she could!"

Kill him twice. Once for you, once for me, Lilith purred, and her words had my hand moving toward her before I even realized it.

I clenched my fingers into fists, dropped my hand

and folded my arms. Reyhan squeaked and I put her on the floor, where she shifted back to two feet and looked around the room. "Where are we?" She sneezed. "It's dusty as shit here."

Lila snickered and I shook my head. Not my kid, I wasn't going to correct her. It was dusty as shit.

"A place to rest for a bit. Maybe get some sleep." I patted her on the head and then sat down with my back against the wall and my feet and face taking in the heat of the flames. She sat next to me and mimicked how I sat.

The shadows danced and flickered against the walls, and the space slowly heated up with the bodies of the horses and the small fire.

Lila rolled on the floor at my feet, dustbathing on the cave's loose sandy floor where it was already heating up. "Maybe you can make a deal with him?" she offered. "He would know a lot about Asag, and before the forbidding thingy that Mamitu talked about that cut the two deserts in half. Maybe he isn't bound by the same rules that she was."

I winked at her, knowing exactly what she was up to, and she winked back. She was setting him up for me to knock him down. "He doesn't know anything, Lila. He's been locked up in a damn vessel at the bottom of a river for like a million years."

"Maybe even a billion billion." Reyhan curled up beside me, yawning. "A long time."

I wrapped an arm around her, and she snuggled

against my side, her breathing shifting into one that spoke of a deep sleep. I would never understand how kids could sleep in such weird positions.

"The kid has a point, it was so long ago, he likely doesn't know," Lila said. "Or maybe wouldn't remember even if he did. He's old. You remember how it was with your grandfather. Couldn't believe a thing he said." The flames cast shadows over her purple and blue scales.

"Good points," I said, though I wished she hadn't brought up my grandfather. He was the last person I wanted to think about.

Vahab was quiet.

I pulled food and a flask out of the saddlebags and made myself eat a bit of dried meat and slurped back a bit of the melted ice water. Hardly what I would call satisfying, but it would do. I woke Reyhan up and had her eat some too, and then she was right back to sleep.

Closing my eyes, I waited. I don't know how long passed, but I rested and the flames at my feet guttered into nothing but embers before Vahab spoke again.

"I can . . . guide you. Perhaps," he said finally. "But I wish to be free. No more bindings on me."

I cracked one eye open and glanced down. "And what if Asag finds you? I'm assuming he is the one who stuffed you in the bottle the first time?"

A grunt rumbled the container on my hip. "He was not the one who stuffed me in here."

I did, Lilith said, and then she laughed.

The container rumbled against me as if Vahab were

pissed off and shaking his fist at me, as if he could hear Lilith too.

I frowned. No, that rumble hadn't been on my hip. I put a hand to the ground and the shaking came through my palm.

"Everyone, quiet," I whispered. I slowly got to my feet and in the semi-darkness put saddles and bridles back on the two horses. Just as silently I lifted Reyhan up in my arms, pushed my alpha's power into her tiny body and forced her to shift to her jungle cat form.

I set her on Balder's back and patted his neck while she blinked sleepily at me. "Be ready, friend."

He bumped me with his nose and gave me a quick bob of his head.

The rumbling was intensifying now, drawing closer. Big enough to be trouble, whatever it was.

"Answer me—" Vahab grumped, and I pressed a hand to the container as if I could squeeze his neck.

"We have company. Be quiet. We'll finish this conversation later." I gave a low growl, hating that I had to speak at all.

That steady thumping rumble kept on coming. Whatever it was, was now inside the cavern with us with the shuffling and scuffing of dirt that rippled our way.

Fuck, shit, damn, piss on my boots. The urge to reach for Lilith tightened every muscle in me and about strangled my ability to breathe. But I didn't touch the sword handle. I knew this game; I'd played it long enough with the sister weapon—my flail. I had to be stronger than her, that was all.

I made a motion for Lila, and she flew to my shoulder. "Any ideas?"

She drew a deep breath and then coughed. "Dragon."

That was not good. Because all the dragons here belonged to Asag as far as I knew.

The other important part of this was that sneaking up on dragons was a terrible idea in general. Maybe we were in her lair? That was more of a double fuck. Territorial didn't even begin to describe dragons. Not even close.

Grimacing, I cleared my throat. One chance. To call out and hope we didn't end up trying to fight our way past it.

"Not to be rude, but is this your home?" I said.

The thumping stopped and I made my feet move, stepping out and around the curve of the tunnel to where I could see the entrance, my hands spread wide at my waist, showing that we had no weapons. The light was still dim. I would have been able to see the entrance had there not been an enormous, sinewy body in front of us blocking the natural light of the land.

The dragon blinked down at me, blood running from a wound in its head that colored through some of the white mane that rolled and fluffed out around its head like a lion. That same flowing white rolled down its long spine.

Eyes of deepest green, like a forest at night just kind of locked onto me. Not menacing, not angry, just . . . watching.

Bronzed horns protruded back, curving like branches from a tree, brushing the ceiling of the cave. Dark green scales covered the midsection of its body and a glittery, opalescent white scale flashed on its underbelly.

Clawed front and back legs in the same bronze tones of the horns dug into the floor of the cave. The steady drip of blood falling from its head was the only sound.

Well, not quite.

Lila was snarling under her breath. "Get out. This is our cave! You don't belong here! Monster!"

I reached up and put a hand on her, and those dark green eyes tracked my movement. Shit, Lila losing her mind was not what we needed right then. I was doing my best not to freak out because the dragon's mouth was only about two feet from my midsection. And I was not so stupid as to think that even wounded, this dragon would be slow. The sinuous movement was all muscle.

He would strike and I would never see it coming at this range.

"It is not my home." His voice was deep, and

melodic, and a little uncertain. "I am injured and wish to stay until the storm passes. That is all I ask."

"No." Lila leapt from my shoulder, flying straight into the dragon's face so they were nose to nose. "No. You can't stay here! Get the fuck out!"

I grabbed her by the tail and dragged her back. "Lila, he's hurt." And he could kill us without a lot of effort. I wanted her to hear what I wasn't saying. We couldn't afford to fight him.

She was vibrating and didn't take her eyes off the new dragon. "I don't care. I know about *your* kind. I know that you hunt other dragons!" She was screeching and her mouth was foaming at the lips. As if acid was bubbling...

"Shit!" I jumped away from her as the acid *did* drip, sizzling as it hit the ground.

The green dragon pulled back a little, eyes widening. "I will leave." I took note that he didn't deny her words.

Lila snorted at him, hovering in midair. "Away, be gone! Hence, be gone, away!"

That she was spitting Shakespeare at him was no surprise. I found it interesting which play it was from.

A slow breath rolled from between his teeth. "Oh, I am fortune's fool."

Lila hissed, still spitting acid.

The thing with me was I had pretty decent instincts. I mean, not perfect, but pretty good. And my impression of the green dragon? He wasn't going to be a problem. Despite what Lila thought.

He was at the mouth of the tunnel before I pulled it together. "Stay. Just don't come further into the tunnel. You'll die if you go back out there."

As if to highlight my words, an ice ball the size of my head slammed into the front edge of the cave, sending shards every which way.

Lila got in front of me, glaring, acid still dripping, and then turned away. I don't think I'd ever seen her so angry—at least not with me. Not in all the times we'd argued about stuff, this felt . . . different. She shot past me back toward the horses and the still sleeping Reyhan. "You have no idea, shifter! No idea what you've done!"

Ouch.

The green dragon backed a few steps away from the entrance, closer toward me, limping. Each step rumbled through the ground. "I give you, my thanks."

I tipped my head at him.

"I am Zamira. That was Lila. Is she right about you killing other dragons?"

He bowed his head to me, his mane fluttering like silk. "I am Fen. The storm caught me unawares and this cave was the first cover I could see." Nice, not answering the hard question.

I nodded. "Us too. Now to the bit about the dragons. You go about killing them?"

He tucked his body in tight, just far enough in that

he wasn't getting many of the shards of still bouncing ice balls. The light had changed a little, and it looked like dawn was coming on, but it was hard to be sure.

The ice had left a thick layer on the ground with well over a foot of frozen shattered pieces piled up.

"Yes and no." He shrugged, his body rippling with the movement. "When needed, my family has hunted other dragons that have caused . . . problems. Dragons that cause problems tend to cause problems for the rest of us if not caught and dealt with quickly."

I snorted. "And you never thought to come after Corvalis?" Corvalis was Lila's father and the biggest, baddest dragon of them all. Or he had been before Lila finished him off and stopped his reign of terror.

Fen's eyes narrowed. "I know that name only in whispers. Is he real?"

"*Was* real," I said. "His daughter killed him when he sought her life, and the life of her chosen family."

He pulled his long tail around his body, curling up tight like a snake coiled, ready to strike. The image in my head made me take a few steps back but he didn't twitch toward me. "That is good. If he was as terrible as the stories, then his daughter is a hero. I would thank her if I could."

I smiled even though said hero was pissed as a wet cat right now. "I agree. She's a badass."

The staccato of the ice falling eased only a little. I realized then we'd been shouting to be heard over it.

"You must have gotten lucky to last this long out there." I swept a hand toward the opening to the cave.

He gave me a toothy smile. "Something like that." A wince and he lifted a clawed hand to his head. "Perhaps not as lucky as I would have liked."

The container hanging from my hip thumped once and the lid rattled. Fen eyed it up. "Did that just . . . move on its own?"

It was my turn to shrug. "Jinn in a bottle. Forgive me, but I have things I must attend to."

And now I would deal with Vahab.

Time to strike a deal with a devil.

3

Here's the thing, what I did know about Vahab was that he was a slippery as fuck, kind of shithead Jinn. What I didn't know was that he'd been playing me.

Goddess damn me to the Witch's Reign and back, he'd been *playing me,* and he was so slick I'd not even picked up on it—my bullshit meter had to be broken. He'd been biding his time. I should have bound him the second that Lilith made the offer, should have forced him to swear on her blade.

Should have, could have, would have.

The second I turned my back on Fen, the dragon was on me. I didn't even have time to scream. His big taloned foot slammed me face first into the dirt and the container was ripped from my side.

"Sorry, he's my boss," Fen said with a legitimate sorrow to his voice. "I don't actually want to do this."

Okay, so maybe my instincts about people were shittier than I'd thought. Fuck me sideways with a cactus, this was not going to help the day start out on a good note.

"Lila!" I screamed for her as I thrashed, barely able to even flex my back, never mind reach for my weapon. I breathed in a mouthful of sand as I pushed with all I had—still to no avail.

A whoosh of wings, and then there was a grunt from the big dragon. His talons lifted off me just enough that I pulled free and yanked Lilith from my back. The blood lust surged through me as I scrambled up to my feet and took in the very new scene.

Vahab shook himself free of the container that was crushed under Fen's left front foot. He was dressed all in black from his thin pants to his knee-high boots and long-sleeved shirt. Dark hair was shorn short at the edges and long at the top. The only color on him at all was the dark green of his eyes. The same green as Fen's scales.

Scratch marks scored Fen's face and from Lila's small claws, there dripped blood. Not hers. His.

"They're working together?" she screeched as she swung away from Fen and back toward me, fury rolling off her. Fen looked . . . uncomfortable.

"Looks like it." I kept the blade pointed at Fen and my eyes on Vahab.

The blood lust was singing hot, and I gritted my teeth against the urges rushing through me. The ease at which Lilith would cut through sinew and bone had me trembling with the need to kill them both and chop them into tiny bits. Adrenaline coursed alongside the urges, and it took all I had to speak through the pulsing energies.

"Get. Back. In. There." I snapped a finger, then pointed at the container at Fen's feet. Broken it may be, but it would still hold him. It had to.

The Jinn . . . he just grinned at me.

"Saucy, aren't you? Did you really think you stuffed me back in that container? That I'd cower before you?" He strolled over to Fen and patted him on the neck. "Good boy. Well done. I knew they'd fall for the injured pet. Women are so very predictable."

Fen's eyes closed a little and he winced. At least he had the grace to be uncomfortable around his boss's sexism.

Vahab put his hands on his hips. "That little friend of mine, that pet of Mamitu's, when he let me out there was no putting me back. But you intrigue me. Which, before you ask, is why I 'let'," he air quoted the word, "you put me back in the container."

His eyes roved over me. I wasn't even sure that it was sexual. Maybe like he said, he was just intrigued.

But then he smiled and lifted his eyebrows at me.

Fuck, it was sexual.

He didn't want to kill me. With a trembling arm I put Lilith back into her sheath.

He will want you now. Let him chase you. Then kill him when he sleeps.

I let go of the handle and the shaking in my arm eased. I flexed my fingers. "So, you fooled me, both of you fooled me. Good job. Why don't you go and kill Asag for revenge? That would be helpful."

Lila backwinged until she sat on my shoulder. She was shaking too, but I had no doubt it was sheer anger and frustration. I could almost feel the emotions between her and me once more. But Asag had taken those too, that connection and bond that we'd made.

Vahab laughed. "Ah, well, I could do that. But what's the fun of it? I'd rather see what you're up to, Spicy. Follow you around. I've not been out of that container in what feels like forever. And I knew that if I went back into that container for a time, then I'd be with you." He winked as if we had a secret between us already. "Spicy."

Fuck. That had the feel of a nickname I was not going to like.

I looked past Fen's coiled body. The ice had stopped falling and day had arrived. I gave a low whistle and Balder trotted up and out of the cavern, Dancer behind him. "Lila. I'm sorry. I should have listened to you."

"Forgiven," she muttered. "Let's go."

"Ahh, you have a mount for me even," Vahab purred and reached for Balder.

Balder pinned his ears and snapped his teeth at the Jinn.

I stepped closer to Vahab and jammed a finger into his chest, forcing him to stumble back. "No. No touching me, no touching my friends." Then I continued walking past him. Maybe I should have been afraid of him, I had every reason to be. He was the first Jinn. Dangerous enough that Asag stuck him in a container and dropped him at the bottom of a river.

Dancer caught up to me and I scooped up Reyhan, holding her on my hip as we stepped out into the open air.

The ice shards crunched under each step. There was no way we could go quiet, or fast. At least not until the day's heat melted some of it off.

Here I thought I could just walk away from Vahab.

I didn't think that he'd really follow me around like he'd said, and so I'd ignore him, and he'd just go away.

Wrong again, girl, wrong again.

"Walking? Excellent, I think I would look forward to a walk around the desert, it's been so long since I've truly been able to stretch my legs." Vahab moved as if to step up beside me. I sidestepped and put Balder between us.

I didn't pull myself up onto Balder's back. The ice across the ground was too thick to make it safe. Instead, I led the way on foot, just as Vahab had said.

Lila clutched my shoulder harder than usual. "I told you not to trust him."

I sighed. "I'm sorry. I didn't get a bad vibe off Fen,

and even now he doesn't seem all that pleased with helping Vahab."

"Being on a first-name basis with the bad guys is a terrible idea and giving them excuses is even worse," Lila snapped.

I raised one hand in surrender, still holding Reyhan in the other arm. "Yeah, I can see that."

Reyhan pointed at Dancer, silently asking to get on her horse. I lifted her onto Dancer's back where the little girl shifted to four legs and curled up in the saddle, changed her mind and went back to two legs, all in the matter of a few blinks. From behind us came a solid gasp.

"A shifter that keeps clothes between forms. How?" Vahab's voice was awestruck.

I didn't look back at Vahab. "A necklace in my case." Not really the necklace that did the job, but he didn't need to know that.

"Yes, but what bloodlines? This is amazing!"

I didn't want to tell him and hadn't planned on it. I also hadn't planned on the five-year-old telling him.

"Jinns and shifters make it niftier," Reyhan sang out.

I leapt up onto Balder's back and turned him around. Vahab stood there with Fen. Only Fen wasn't big Fen.

He was *little* Fen, and he was coiled around Vahab's neck and shoulders. Kind of like Lila did with me.

I didn't like the mirror image as Lila tightened her hold on my shoulders. "I don't like that," she hissed.

I didn't know what to make of this situation. Mamitu, guardian of the desert, had made it sound like Vahab would need to be contained. That he was dangerous. And despite not letting him out and negotiating with him, he didn't actually seem all that pissed off.

I was curious about how Fen found us, and how they were tied together after all these years.

No. Bad. Curiosity killed the cat.

I didn't want to be that cat.

"Goodbye, Vahab," I said as I spun Balder and urged him forward.

Dancer leapt with us, Reyhan squealing with delight. Balder plunged and gave a few bucks in utter excitement.

What I didn't expect was a third horse joining us. One with a dark black-green tint to his coat and a long white mane and tail. Or tiny golden horns between his ears.

"What the actual fuck—"

"Oh, don't be crass, Spicy, I don't like a foul mouth in my women." Lilith let out a stream of insults one on top of the other so rapidly I could barely make sense of them even though they were inside my head. However, I did agree with the general vibe. He could take his self-righteous views and stuff them where the sun doesn't shine.

"Fen can take a few different forms," Vahab continued on, oblivious to Lilith's rant. He rode alongside me for a few strides from the back of the horse that had been a dragon only a few moments before. Fen galloped alongside Balder and Dancer, his body still kind of sinewy even though he was technically a horse, which made for an undulating movement that was rather mesmerizing. I shook it off and stared at Vahab. There was no way he'd be able to keep up if I loosened my hold on Balder. If I urged my hornless unicorn forward.

Which I did.

I kissed at Balder, and he took off, Dancer only a half-step behind. Our speed increased with each stride the horses took and Reyhan was squealing with delight as we raced along.

"Faster, faster!" she squealed as the horses stretched out, eating up the ground.

I closed my eyes and breathed in the desert, doing what I could to put the night behind us, and focusing on what was ahead.

Maks. We would find Maks, take him back from the Storm Queen and then figure out the next step toward Asag.

The wind already warmed my face as the heat of the day rose with each passing minute and the last of the ice and water was evaporating. That was the desert for you, water and cold just didn't last. I hoped that the Storm Queen choked on the dust.

I glanced over my shoulder to see Fen fading in the distance, struggling to even keep within sight.

"You really going to just set the first Jinn ever back on the world?" Lila shouted to be heard over the horses' hoofbeats and the whip of wind around us.

"I have enough problems," I shouted back. "So, if he wants to dick around in the desert, thinking he can keep up with us, he is welcome to go ahead and try."

Lila's claws clutched at me. "What if Asag catches him? What if he becomes a weapon against us? I hate to say it, but he seems to kind of like you. I mean . . . maybe we could use that? You could string him along . . .."

I groaned and pulled lightly on Balder's reins, slowing him. Hating that Lila was speaking with some serious reason. "What about Fen? You hate him. Maybe you should string him along then, huh?"

"Well of course I hate him, that won't change," she huffed. "But you're right, we have enough problems. Adding the Jinn to it . . . well, at least if they are with us then they aren't against us? Right?"

That last bit was a tough one for me to swallow. Betrayal was something we'd both known. The two horses slowed to a walk and Fen's hoofbeats could be heard as he approached full speed.

We could outrun them and be done with them. There was no way they'd catch us. But Lila wasn't wrong. I lifted a hand to my back and touched one finger to Lilith's handle, wondering if she had anything to say about the situation.

If he's interested in bedding you, then he will stick around. Don't let him know you have a mate and he'll be good to you. The minute he knows you are not reachable, that's when he'll become dangerous.

Awesome.

"We stay on our toes. No trusting them. We can't slip up for even a second," I said quietly, with half an eye on Reyhan. Not that I didn't trust her, but the kid was sharp as they came, and I realized that speaking freely in front of her could, and had, gotten me into trouble.

Balder came to a halt and pawed at the ground, immediately irritated that we'd stopped. I patted his neck. "What do you think, friend? We good to trust them?"

He flipped his head once and snorted. No emotions or words came through him either as they once had. Damn it all.

Asag had really crimped our style, stealing all our mojo.

"Say nothing about Maks," I murmured to Lila, turning slightly away from Reyhan. "That will send him into a rage."

"Okay." She gripped the edge of my ear as Fen and Vahab rode up beside us. Fen was breathing hard and Vahab was laughing.

"I knew you couldn't resist. Curiosity, am I right?"

He patted his chest. "You wonder what beats here, under my breastbone, is it a heart made for you?"

I rolled my eyes and struggled not to scoff out loud. Instead, I gave him as much truth as I dared. "I don't want Asag getting a hold of you. And as far as I know, he and his cronies are following us."

Vahab looked over his shoulder. "Hmm. Is he still trying to rule the east?"

"Rules the east," I corrected him, then clucked to Balder, who picked up a quick trot.

Fen could keep pace now, though I doubted his stamina would be as good as the horses'.

"I suppose you have many questions?" Vahab asked. "I have many answers but let me guess at what you'd like to know."

Lila spun around and gave me wide eyes. This was . . . unusual. I'd really expected him to be more of a pain in my ass, to be honest.

I shouldn't have been so sure he wouldn't become a pain in my ass. He was, after all, a Jinn.

4

MAKS

"Your mate did not survive the ice storm I swept through the desert. Now you can let her memory go and fuck me as you should."

The words rebounded in his head; they wouldn't absorb into him because it wasn't possible that Zam was not in this world anymore. He would have felt her loss. Maks held perfectly still, barely breathing as the Storm Queen paced in front of him.

"The ice storm destroyed the entire southern range of the desert." She smirked. "So now there is no reason for your loyalty to waver. You are free of her. Then perhaps you can find your passion for my body and give me the child I desire."

His heart thumped hard inside his chest, as if it would climb out and make its way to wherever Zam was, dead or alive. He gritted his teeth. "My loyalty to my mate does not end on her death."

She patted him on the head. "I think you are foolish. Do you know that I have been kind to you thus far?"

He didn't dare look down at the marks on his body, the welts from the whips, the blood streaking his wrists and ankles. All because he couldn't get it up around her. Because if anything, she made him recoil in horror, killing any natural instinct of his dick to twitch around a beautiful, naked woman. There was no lust from him even for her lithe and willing body.

Her sigh filled the bedroom. "I will be kinder yet. I think you are perhaps the strongest Jinn I've met, and I *will* have your child. Which means perhaps I need to employ a . . . different tactic."

Her fingers traced along the underside of his jaw, scratching her nails until they dug into the soft spot under his chin. She tipped his head up with one hand and snapped her fingers with the other. "Bring it to me and be quick about it."

It. What was this now? He dared a look around, without moving his head.

Movement from the corner of the room, and Maks fully expected it to be one of her thugs come to beat him again and then throw him into a new cell. Maybe one with hot lava or spikes. As if that would make a man aroused.

But it was not one of the usual thugs. A slim, aged woman shuffled forward. Her silvery white hair was wild, as if she'd been caught in the wind, and her limbs were thin like old sticks broken from a dying tree. Her eyes were sharp, though, and full of intelligence that hovered on the edge of madness.

"My queen," she whispered with a lisp, while she bent at the waist, something in her hands offered up. "A potion of the rabisu's song. He will see only the one he loves when he looks on you."

Fuck.

He clamped his mouth shut and the Storm Queen laughed softly. "Oh, as if closing your mouth will stop me from forcing this into you. Foolish boy."

She tipped his head back further and he tightened his jaw. Of course, he didn't expect her to give up easily, but neither would he. She clamped a hand on the back of his head, so he was arched hard and as far as his back would allow against the bonds that held him, and then she jammed the thin tube into his nostril, tipping it so the potion was in him in a matter of seconds.

Coughing and spluttering, he choked as it ran down the back of his throat. Coppery, it tasted of blood and the faint tang of sharp herbs. His eyes watered and his body spasmed, dancing and jerking as the potion took hold of him, flooding through his veins and sinking deep into his bones.

Her hands left him as he struggled to breathe, still coughing, spitting to the side. The bindings came off him and he slid down until he lay belly first on the cold tile floor. Vision fuzzing, he didn't move as he tried to figure out if he could fight this potion.

She didn't care if she killed him, not really. If he'd died right there, choking on the fluid she herself had shoved into him, it wouldn't have mattered to her. And that was the danger of this one. If he died, she'd be upset for about half a minute and then she would hunt for another male Jinn.

His life was nothing to her, he was replaceable.

You need to fool her, boy. You need to placate her long enough to escape. Zam will understand that you had no choice. Survival is the key here. Survive.

Marsum's voice was strong in his head. Strong and sad. Perhaps more than any other person alive, Marsum knew just how much Maks loved his mate. They'd shared a body and Marsum had been inside his head, had seen how deep that connection was. And now the only way to get back to her was to . . . be with another woman. He didn't think he could do it. He couldn't betray her that way, not even for his life, as foolish as that was. The Storm Queen was not going to have him if he had any say over it.

"Well, pet?" she purred. "What do you think now?"

The Storm Queen stood right in front of him, her toes right by his hands. He could have grabbed her by the ankles and thrown her against the wall. He could have shifted and made a run for it. But . . . if his timing was off, he'd be dead in seconds.

Could he placate her long enough to find a way out? She would know, though, unless he could give her a better act than Shakespeare had ever penned.

He pushed slowly to his hands and knees; head hung low as his breath came in deep pants. He could do this thing that horrified him—he could make her believe that she was the one he wanted, just long enough to get free.

The fluid flowed through him, and his mind grew fuzzy, as if he were drinking țuică. He blinked and lifted his hands to his face, wobbling where he stood.

Her hands touched his, the skin rough, callused. Like Zam's. He stared at her hands, seeing the scars and marks that came from surviving. Marks he knew so well.

"You can't be Zam. How?"

"Oh, but I am." And damn it if it didn't sound like his mate. The slight edge to her words, the bits of gravel that he'd always found so damn sexy.

He lifted his head slowly, starting at her feet and going up her legs. Legs that he knew, the same as the hands that held his. Startled, he fell backward as he stared into the green eyes that he loved. Green eyes that he would know anywhere.

"Hurry," she whispered and held out a hand. "I can't hold the Storm Queen back for long. She is too strong even for me."

The potion sunk into him further and he lifted his hand, setting it in her fingers. Feeling the hands that he'd kissed, that had run over his body, now they clung to him and dragged him upward. Took him out of this place. Zam would save him as she'd done before.

He forgot everything but her. His mate. His heart. Forgot that there was a magic pulsing in his blood.

The liquid in his veins flowed thicker, pushing its way into every part of him, pulsing in his throat and tightening the muscles. His vision narrowed to the woman he loved and nothing more.

Not even Marsum spoke to him.

Zam pulled him along behind her, stopping at intersections of the palace, keeping him safe as guards strode by, pressing her body against his as she hid them both. Up and up, they went. To the top of the palace, to the rooftop where they could escape.

On the parapet of the roof, Lila was perched, waiting, her eyes tracking them as they ran across to her.

"Lila," he mumbled, expecting her to call him Toad. To tell him to hurry his ass up. But she was silent. Waiting.

Zam continued to drag him along, and he tried to keep up, stumbling across the roof. Why was he so slow? His legs felt as though he wore shackles. But Zam didn't argue. She didn't berate him. She just pushed him up onto Lila's back. "Hurry, we have to hurry. We can't slow down, not for an instant. Trust me."

He nodded and held a hand to her. She jumped up onto Lila's back and in a single push of the dragon's wings and legs, they were off.

Lila felt . . . strange. Softer than before. As if she were made of feathers and not tough, leathery skin. He pressed a hand against her body and the image fuzzed, showing him tawny, golden fluff for a split second before it slid back to dragon hide. "Lila, what's wrong?"

Before the dragon could answer him, before he could question the fact that she was able to shift sizes once more, Zam twisted around to face him.

"Maks, kiss me," she whispered, sliding her hands over his shoulders and down his chest before she offered her face up to him, lips slightly parted.

With a low growl he pulled her back tight against his chest, and kissed her hard, not caring that they were in the air, that Lila would tease them later. He didn't care. This was his mate. And she'd rescued him from that bitch of a Storm Queen. And he wanted to touch and taste every inch of her body. His hands slid under her shirt, across smooth, scarless skin.

Scarless. That seemed . . . wrong.

The wind howled around them, the smell of the ocean crisp and clear as he kissed her deeper and deeper until she was moaning. Her hands tangled around his clothes, as if she would pull them off right there.

Lila landed and Zam pulled back, flushed and panting. "Goddess. You are a charm, aren't you?"

He leaned to kiss her again, and a look of fear flashed across her face right before she all but pushed him off Lila's back. "That's a good boy. I can't let you get too close."

He grinned, tried to speak but his words were slurred. His mouth stumbling like his feet meant that no words came out. Why wouldn't she want him close? He blinked and again the world fuzzed. For a moment they were back on the castle that they'd just left, and then it twisted and turned into a different building, one that was more like a house on the edge of the sea.

"Too close," he mumbled. They were too close to the water. The water was where the Storm Queen was.

Zam laced her fingers with his and pulled him after her once more. Down flight after flight of stairs. Too many for a house this size. His mouth might have been struggling to speak, and his eyes were fuzzed with something, but his brain was starting to work once more. His mind and heart tried to free him from . . . whatever this was.

He counted the flights of stairs. The house had been one level.

They went down eight flights of stairs.

The sluggishness in his veins slid a little and the figure in front of him shimmered, going from the woman he loved, to the Storm Queen and back again. How?

Scarless. There were no scars and that wasn't . . ..

"Zam?" He managed to get her name out.

"Come on, pet, almost there." She purred. Purred. That seemed . . . not right. He knew that Zam could purr in her house cat form but never when she was on two legs.

She put her shoulder to a door and then backed through, drawing him with her. A bed dominated the room, a fire burned in a brazier in the corner, the smell of fresh bread, a simmering pot of meat and spices—curry maybe—it all pulled him forward.

"You can eat after, pet. I want you inside of me. Now. Make me yours."

Zam stripped her clothes away in a flurry and then set to work on his, yanking them from him. He stood still and let her; eyes half closed, letting the sensations roll over him. Barely able to breathe through the uncertainty that was stealing whatever sense of rightness had been there even moments before.

"Slow," he whispered and even that word was harder yet. His brain and body were trying to tell him something. This was wrong. So wrong. They needed to not hurry this for some reason he couldn't put his fingers on.

"Oh, we can go as slow as you like, pet." She went up on her toes, pressing her breasts against his bare chest. He should have been ecstatic. He'd never bedded Zam in a proper bed with cushions and a mattress. Yet his body was unmoved.

She nipped the side of his neck, kissed his earlobe and sucked it into her mouth as her hands dipped to lower regions, stroking and touching.

A groan slid from him as his head tipped back. It felt good. It felt wrong. He started to shake.

This was . . . not right.

And the only thing he could think was that maybe if he just went to sleep, he'd wake up and this would be a dream, a strange dream that felt all too real. He managed to get his hands up, and press them into her upper arms, holding her still.

Fighting the grogginess, the fuzzing of his eyes, he stared down into her green ones. "Slow, Zam, go slow."

She blew out a breath and rolled her eyes but followed him as he stumbled toward the bed. It was his turn to drag her down to the cushions and she fell on top of him, straddling his hips, working her way over him as he grew harder.

He kept his eyes closed. Breathed through the sensations. Tried to pinpoint what was so wrong about this moment. He put his hands on her hips and held her tight to keep her from moving.

"Pet, I want you to fuck me." Her words were sharp, and he felt the sting of them, like a lash. He opened his eyes. Strike that. She *had* lashed him with a leather strap.

He rolled, pinning her arms with ease, and holding her tight. "Sleep. Sex later."

"Oh, my goddess, no! We are not sleeping!" She fought against him, and he lifted an arm, setting her free. He wouldn't make her stay. She'd come sleep beside him when she was tired. Lila would curl up between them and then bitch about smelling lusting hormones all night.

He smiled and his breathing slowed as his body sunk into—not a slumber, that would mean he was sleeping, and he could still hear what was going on around him. Some kind of fog was what he was in.

"Why did the potion not work?"

"Mistress, I do not know! It has been a proven potion on male Jinn for generations. There must be—"

"Something you did wrong! You've ruined this!" Zam screamed. Only . . . was it Zam? Her voice was off now.

"Mistress, this is not the first time I've created this potion. I assure you that there is nothing wrong with it." The one who answered was sharp and unafraid of the screaming woman who maybe wasn't Zam.

"Pissed," Maks mumbled under his breath. The unafraid one was pissed.

"Then what is it?" Zam snapped. "Why isn't he reacting the same way? Why isn't he fucking the ever-living goddess out of me?"

A hand touched his back, though 'hand' was a loose description as the fingers felt more like skeletal talons. "Something about *him* is the issue . . ." The fingers dug in, and he groaned as the pain pushed the fog back. "Perhaps he is not quite what he seems?"

Shift. What if he shifted? Would that help him?

No. He swallowed the urge down. Shifting now would tip his hand and he was hanging onto that until he was sure he could escape. He had to wait for the moment . . . but why was he trying to escape Zam?

"Something . . ." The talon fingers dug deeper, drawing another low moan out of him and his skin rippled as he fought another wave of needing to shift. "Ah. You see that? He is not pure."

"WHAT?" The screech filled the air, cutting through the last of the drink that she—the Storm Queen—had given him. His mind cleared rapidly, as though he'd been dunked in ice water, but he stayed where he was. "He's not . . . pure? What the fuck does that mean?"

"That is what I said," the scratchy voice answered. "Not pure. A mutt. A half-breed. Your child would also then not be pure."

The screams reverberated through the room, and he made himself lie still. Waiting.

As they subsided, a sob rippled from her, the weight of her settling onto the bed and for a moment he felt sorry for her. The shaking of her crying sent ripples through even the thick mattress.

"I shall never have a child." She drew a sucking breath, and the sorrow in her voice was thick, wet with tears. "I shall never hold my own child."

He reached for her, his hand hovering at her lower back. Uncertain. Not that he would be the one to give her a child, but her pain drew him as her demands could not have.

Her back stiffened before his hand landed and she stood. She didn't look back at him as she spoke.

"He is of no use to me. Kill him."

Well fuck, so much for feeling sorry for her.

"Asag, the Beast from the East," Vahab almost sung the words as we rode south. Toward the Sea of Storms and the Queen who had Maks. What a damn mess my life was. Not that it was any surprise to me or anyone who knew me.

My hands tightened on the reins and my jaw ticked. That bitch was going to get her ass handed to her on the end of my sword. Lilith whispered encouragement from my back. *I will help with that. Gladly. I don't like men stealers.*

"What about him?" Lila asked. "Or do you just get a kick out of saying his name like that?"

She clung to the front of my saddle, glaring across at Fen and Vahab.

Vahab saluted her. "He is a demon, and he is lazy which will be his downfall one day. He likes Jinn women; they are his flavor, if you will. But he likes them young." His eyes slid over me and then rested on Reyhan. "So, you two would be a draw regardless of the fact that you have released me and are now trapezing across the desert that he likely considers his own."

I wasn't sure I'd call it a desert now, at least not the sandy desert that I was used to. The ground was hard, cracked, completely baked from the heat of the sun. "The way to him is across the mountains," Lila said. "And we are headed south which means he won't be looking our way. We are fooling him."

"Says the dragon who knows nothing about this side of the desert." Fen snorted and shook his head, so his mane flipped every which way. "You are ignorant, little girl."

Oh, those was fighting words if I ever heard them.

Lila surprised me, though; she didn't speak to him, just shot up into the air, her body vibrating. "I'm going to scout ahead. I do smell all horse piss, at which my nose is in great indignation."

"Good idea, Tempest." I arched a brow, and she gave me a subtle nod. She was okay, just furious. As long as she wasn't hurt by him. The fact that she threw out a Shakespeare quote was interesting.

He didn't so much as blink at it.

I glanced over at Fen who trotted alongside us after she flew away. "You're a dick, you know that, right."

"Dick, dick, he's a dick!" Reyhan sing-songed from Dancer's back, making me smile.

Fen stared straight ahead. "She is young and a fool

to think that no one has noticed your passing. You *both* are fools to think that because you have come this far, you will make it safely. And then to bring a child with you is beyond—"

"Enough." Vahab put a hand to Fen's neck and the dragon went silent. "You are half shifter, like the girl?"

I nodded. I wasn't going to defend bringing Reyhan with us. I'd leave her behind the first chance I got if there was safety for her. And I certainly wasn't about to tell Vahab that I was a granddaughter of the Emperor. Nope, that was a bad idea. So, I changed the subject from me, back to the issue at hand. "Tell me what you know of Asag."

Vahab sighed. "Honestly, there is not much to tell. He was a powerful demon when he was called across to this land. That much has not changed by the sounds of it. He draws his power by eating the power and magic of others. If he has been here for many generations, then there will not be many left that have any magic, so to speak."

Balder shook his head and gave a low snort. I thought about the unicorn herds. "Did he take the unicorns for the same reason as he takes the dragons?"

Vahab startled. "He took dragons?"

"The hatchlings." I stared at the sky as Lila came hurtling back toward us. Too fast. She was coming in too fast for this to be anything but trouble.

"That's a terrible idea, taking dragons of any sort.

Unless they bond willingly to you, they are always on the cusp of being turned against their master."

Fen gave a low grumble but I couldn't look away from Lila as she all but dive bombed into my arms. The impact drove the wind out of me, and I struggled a moment to breathe as she started yelping.

"Big birds. The rhuk! They'll see us in less than a minute at the speed they're coming in!"

And we were out in the open with no chance for cover. Fen wouldn't be able to keep up as a horse. There weren't a lot of options, and I made my decision in a split second. I didn't doubt that as a full-sized dragon he might be okay, but that didn't leave much for the rest of us.

"You need to get small right now!" I snapped a finger at Fen, and he just stared at me. "Vahab, get on Dancer. Reyhan, come to me." I was already grabbing the girl and dragging her onto Balder's back with me. Her tiny arms wrapped around my middle. We had to run, and we had to run now.

Vahab snorted. "Rhuk? They are no trouble. We need to eat tonight, they are quite lovely with a fresh cream sauce."

I stared at him. "Eat? They're as big as a goddess-favored dragon!"

His eyes widened. "Truly? Last I saw them they were no bigger than a fluff of chickens."

"Give me a flouncing satyr any day over this one," I

whispered to myself. Vahab mounted up on Dancer who took a couple bouncing, bucking steps.

"Lovely, is she always so calm?" He bit out the words between being thrown about.

I ignored him, clutched Reyhan tight and gave Balder his head, knowing that Dancer would keep up with or without her new rider. Balder knew it too. He went from standing still to a flat-out gallop with a single leap. Behind me Vahab yelped, no doubt thrown back in his saddle from the force Dancer exerted in order to keep up with Balder.

"Which direction are they coming from?" I hollered into the wind.

"South. Straight up from the Sea of Storms I'd guess," Lila yelled back as she clung to my shoulder. I leaned forward, keeping Reyhan pinned between me and the saddle.

"Are we in danger?" Reyhan asked, her eyes wide.

I didn't have it in me to lie to her this time. "A little bit. But we're going to try and outrun it. Just hang on."

A niggling along my spine, and Lilith whispered.

We could kill them. Then the child would be safe. We could save her. You need only join me, and our strength would stop them.

Her words sunk into me, trembling along my nerve endings; my eyelids fluttered as my breath hitched on the adrenaline that came not from the speed of my horse, but with the thoughts of a battle. An epic fight. Blood flowing from the bodies of my enemies.

Together we are strong enough. Words, they were just words, and I knew that I should probably do something about how I was feeling, but the feeling of concern ticked away, drop by drop until all thoughts of caution, of fleeing were gone.

"Lila, we have to kill them!" I yelled as the rhuk came into view. They saw us at the same time and angled their big wings toward us. Beaks open. Talons spread wide.

"Are you insane?" Lila screeched right in my ear. "We can outrun them! Why are you slowing Balder down?"

My hands tightened on the reins, yanking Balder to a hard stop. I should have felt bad for it. Should have felt something.

We had to kill them. There was no other way.

Kill them all. We will kill them all.

"All of them," I growled.

Reyhan whimpered and in a blink, she'd shifted into her four-legged shape of a jungle cat cub and leapt off Balder's back.

Vahab hollered from behind me, but his words bounced off me. "Don't let her have you, desert girl! Fight her!"

I lifted my eyes to look into the cloudless sky. The rhuk were growing larger by the second until their tawny, sand-colored feathers were visible.

I reached for the blade on my back as Balder danced sideways. He whinnied, and the sound was shrill as a trumpet.

He didn't want to stand still. He wanted to run.

I yanked his reins again, trying to force him.

"What are you doing?" Lila flew in front of me, her purple eyes wide and scared. She was scared.

I felt . . . nothing.

"Out of my way!" I snarled. "I'll kill them myself!"

She shook her head, eyes darting to the sword. "Oh, camel shit on my wings! You're listening to that damn sword, aren't you? Tap dancing goddess, you have to listen to me!"

Dancer slid to a stop next to us, Vahab grinning like a fool. "Ah, this is almost as good as riding a unicorn!"

I locked my eyes on him and my throat tightened. The two birds coming our way were forgotten.

Cheating filthy bastard.

I lunged out of my saddle, straight for Vahab. "Cheating bastard!"

Vahab's mouth gaped open, and Dancer jigged sideways, so I missed them both and hit the sand face first.

"You have to snap out of it, Zam!"

Lila. Balder. My two friends.

No, I will rule you!

Sweat poured down my face and arms as I wrestled for control of my own body. The whoosh of wings, the scream of the horses, of Reyhan snarling and crying out. I had to pull it together.

I will save them. Stop fighting me! Obey me!

She could not have used a worse word. Steve had said that on too many occasions.

'Why won't you just obey me? Do as you're told! You're my wife, I will tell you who to be!' Steve's voice rolled into Lilith's as she demanded my obedience to her.

"Fuck you!" I rolled to my back, caught a glimpse of feathers and threw the sword straight up and into the belly of the rhuk as it swept toward Balder. The blade stuck deep, burying up to the hilt straight through the ribcage. A lucky shot. A saving throw. A burst of feathers, the bird faltered and let out a gurgling screech.

My horse reared up and struck out with his hooves, knocking the now terribly wounded bird, driving it the rest of the way to the ground away from us.

The second rhuk pulled up and circled around us, its shiny black eyeball giving us some serious stink eye as it tipped its head this way and that. Considering us. Wondering how dangerous we were.

I was on my knees, fingers buried in the sand. A blur of black across the sand caught its stink eye and mine at the same time.

Reyhan. Running scared, because of me.

"No!" I stumbled forward and shifted to my four-legged jungle cat form even as the rhuk flew straight toward the cub.

No. No.

I tore across the sand, eating the distance between us. But I was too far behind. The rhuk dropped down and its massive talons closed around a screeching, spitting Reyhan. The bird was too big to pull straight up which bought me a little time.

Lila shot through the air beside me.

"Can you drive it toward the cliffs?" I yelled.

"Done!" Lila winged away. Where was Fen when we needed help?

The cliffs were to the east of us, bordering the desert. If I could get some height . . .

Maybe all was not lost. Maybe I could make it.

Seconds later I was at the base of the cliffs. Cliffs that no horse could have scaled. But a jungle cat, that was a whole different set of rules.

With a powerful push off my haunches, I leapt straight up a solid twelve feet, claws digging into the sandstone cliffs as I yanked myself up and up. There was no option of failure.

I couldn't let the girl down.

It was my fault she'd been snatched.

I'd pulled Lilith free thinking I was strong enough to take her on, the same way I'd taken on the flail.

Wrong again.

The scrabble of rocks behind me told me I had company coming up fast, but I didn't dare look back. My balance was precarious. Another leap and I was up on top of the lower cliffs.

There was no time for anything but as much speed as I could manage.

Reyhan was screeching and the big rhuk was slowly

being directed toward me. Sort of. The bird was ahead of me, but parallel to the cliff. I just . . . had to catch up.

I dug deep and raced along the cliff top gaining inch by inch as Lila did her damndest to keep the rhuk close to the cliff.

The problem?

I was running out of runway.

I needed more cliffs; I needed more footing.

The rhuk was just ahead of me and off to my left. I was going to have to make a leap of faith and hope that I was not misjudging the distance.

With everything I had in me, I extended myself almost flat to the ground as I covered the last bit of the cliffs in three strides, pushing off and leaping to the left.

The big ass chicken ducked to the right as the cliffs disappeared, putting its body right under me. I landed square on its back and dug my claws in.

"Hang on, Reyhan!"

A screaming caterwaul was the only answer from her.

"I'll try and get her loose!" Lila yelled. "You kill the bird!"

That was my goal. Only the rhuk had taken note of me as my claws dug in deep. It let out a scream, like the sound of a screeching clarinet being played with by a small child oblivious to the horrid noise it was making. Three bursts of a screech and then silence.

More like a call for help than anything else.

Fuck me.

The rhuk rolled suddenly to the left, tucking its wings in tight and spinning hard enough that if I'd not had my claws dug in deep to its flesh I would have been flung out.

As it was, I just dug in harder. A few choice words slipped out of me that rhymed with ducking mother ducking bird.

Hopefully Reyhan didn't hear me.

The rhuk levelled back out, whipped around with its beak and tried to pluck me off. I swatted at its face, avoiding the snapping beak that was filled with teeth. More like a lizard than a bird, it was going for blood now. But I wasn't any less determined.

"Snap its neck like a turkey!"

I didn't look to where Vahab raced along underneath us, though his words carried clear.

Like I didn't know that the neck was the place to bite.

I belly crawled my way up the rhuk's back as I tried to get closer to the neck—my original goal.

What I didn't expect was a bolt of lightning.

Nor for that lightning to hit the bird and in turn hit me.

The arc of brilliant white light slit the sky open and

slammed into the rhuk. The electricity shot through the bird and into me. It shouldn't have hurt me. We weren't on the ground.

But the power inside the electricity was not natural. It felt more like . . . a Jinn's magic as it crawled under my fur and spasmed my muscles and bones right down to the tips of my ears. I breathed it in. Jinn magic for sure. And while I might not have my own magic, I absorbed this as if . . . as if I still had my flail with me. Not enough, though.

Even with that, I barely managed to keep my claws clenched tight as the rest of my body went limp, dangling from the back of the big bird.

My tongue lolled out and I struggled to keep steady. I had to keep steady for Reyhan, I couldn't let go.

"Is she dead *again*?" That voice was familiar, and I knew it belonged to the angel I'd seen both times I'd been near death.

"No, no, I think she's going back on her own." That one belonged to the demonic-looking beasty. Though they had saved me. I tried to see them, tried to ask them why they'd helped me before.

"Seriously, she has to have the worst luck I've ever seen."

"Well, she's a black cat, after all."

The words were gone in a haze. I'd not needed them this time.

Slowly the magic faded, and I blinked. I still hung

from the bird. Could still hear Lila and Reyhan scream back and forth.

Vahab yelled from below us. Balder trumpeted a whinny.

It could have been a minute I was out or an hour. I wasn't sure.

With a snarl I pulled myself up and scrambled along the rhuk's back. The bird squawked and then I was on its neck, my mouth pinning the long narrow vertebrae with my jaws.

Perks to being a jungle cat. My jaws closed down.

I didn't have to wait for someone with bigger teeth to come along and help anymore.

The bird's wings tucked in as if it were going for another dive, but as I squeezed down with my incisors, the snapping of bones reverberated through me as I crushed the spinal cord.

We dropped from the sky like a stone, the rhuk's wings crumpling.

"I got the kid!" Lila yelled, swinging up to where I could see her as I followed the rhuk to the ground.

The impact snapped my mouth off the back of the neck, and I was flung hard out into the loose sand and hard ground. I rolled and came up on two feet in a low crouch, hands on my smaller daggers. Waiting.

The rhuk shuddered and lay still, but the bird's back still rose and fell. It breathed; it was alive.

Hoofbeats and then Balder was there beside me. "I'm sorry." I held out a hand and he gave me a well-deserved snort, flinging snot onto my outstretched fingers. "I deserved that." I wiped my fingers along his mouth where I'd driven the bit into his tender flesh. "I'm sorry, my friend, I never should have taken that damn sword."

Vahab rode up with Dancer. "That was well done. Good thing you listened to me finally and broke the neck. That is the way with birds, you know. Best way to deal with them quick."

"Much help you were," Lila yelped as she slid into view, Reyhan clutched in her claws. She dropped the cub to me, and I held her tight to me until she shifted back to two legs and gave me a hug back.

"I'm sorry," I said. "I'm sorry that I scared you."

"Was that the bad knife?" Reyhan asked.

"It was." Apparently, she'd been more awake during my and Lila's conversations about Lilith than I'd realized.

"You threw it away. So, it's gone now?"

"I did." But already I knew I couldn't leave it in the other rhuk. If the wrong person got a hold of it . . . then we were in serious trouble.

Take, for instance, Asag.

I grimaced just thinking about having to handle Lilith again.

The rhuk behind us let out a gurgling cry.

I lifted Reyhan up onto Balder's back. "I have to give it mercy."

I pulled my shotgun free from the saddle and

checked the chamber. I had two slugs ready to go. Funny how I'd not even thought of the long-range weapon when the rhuk had been bearing down on us. Of course, that could have been Lilith too, keeping me focused on her.

With a sigh I made myself go around to the back of the bird's neck. Like the few large dragons I'd met—Lila included—the creature seemed so much bigger once it was still and on the ground. The wings were at an odd angle, not broken, just spread wide. Its beak was partly open as it struggled to breathe.

"Mercy." The rhuk spoke softly. "You said you'd give me mercy."

I swallowed hard, my willingness to end its life wavering with those words. "Did you have to speak?"

"You thought us dumb creatures? Easier to kill then, yes?" It didn't open its eye but lay still on the ground, struggling to breathe, the gurgling of each breath and effort of drawing it in growing stronger.

"Yes." There was no getting around that truth. And I was no liar. "I'd prefer you just be a monster that needs killing."

It clacked its beak and teeth a single time. "You think that dragons are the only ones caged?"

I went to one knee, behind its head. Probably the safest spot I could be if it was faking its paralysis. One snap of its teeth-encrusted beak could easily cut me in half.

"You? The rhuk? You're caged?"

"The Storm Queen takes the rhuk when they are fledglings. Barely old enough to eat on their own. It's how she holds her own against Asag. That and the fear that she could be the one to end him . . ." The eye opened, and I could see that the solid black held a shimmer of some other color inside of it. This close there were flecks of gold and brown, mimicking the tawny feathers that covered the massive body. "Her power fled me as I fell. She believes me dead and so I am . . . free. Give me mercy. Kill me. Send me to my family beyond the Veil."

I put a hand against the feathers and lifted my blade. There was no way I could save this soul. I'd paralyzed the bird.

A nose pushed against my shoulder, and I looked up to see Balder right behind me. Of anyone else here, he had all the reasons to want the rhuk dead. They hunted the unicorns, feasted on them and gave them over to the Storm Queen.

He bumped me again with his nose, then twisted around to touch the saddlebags across his back. I closed my eyes, knowing what he was getting at. "And if I use the horn that your father gave for you, what next? There is power in it to give you your life back as it was, Balder."

He blew out a snort and pawed the ground, then reached back and all but yanked the saddlebags off. I stood and untied them. "This could be a terrible idea."

Balder snorted and I looked to Lila, who sat quite still on Balder's back. Her eyes were closed.

"Lila, what do you think?"

"I think that no matter what you do, this is a defining moment. Just like bringing Vahab and his pet dumbass with us was." Her eyes opened and she looked at me. "There's small choice in a barrel of rotten apples. I trust you."

I grimaced, agreeing with her and Shakespeare. "Fair."

"Aren't you going to ask me?" Vahab put his hand to his chest.

I blinked over at him. "You? I'm beginning to think you aren't even a Jinn. Why would I ask your opinion?"

His hand splayed wider on his chest. "I am the FIRST Jinn!"

Fen peeked out from around his shoulder riding along with his master the same way Lila did with me. He rolled his eyes and shook his head. Interesting.

But not really my issue I had to deal with in that moment.

I pulled the unicorn horn out, rolling the spiraled horn in my hands. This had been Torin's, and he'd died fighting off a rhuk. The very creature I was considering healing with the horn. He'd given his life so that we could survive, so that we could see these journeys through. What would he say to us saving one of his enemies?

"Fuck," I whispered.

Reyhan cleared her throat. "We don't say fuck here."

"Well, you don't," I muttered as I knelt back by the rhuk's head. "If I heal you, will you fly away, far enough away to stay safe from the Storm Queen?"

The rhuk rolled its big eye to me. "Why?"

"Cause I'm a fuc—freaking genius," I said with a quick glance at Reyhan. "I don't know, okay? I listen to my horse. He's a good boy and he said to save you."

"You trust him," the bird mumbled. "As a pair together should trust one another."

I didn't know really what it was mumbling about, but kind of got the drift. "Yes or no. That's the question."

"Yes. If I can live and be free, I choose life."

I laid the horn tip against the bird's neck, pushing it through the feathers until it touched bare skin. A flare of light burst outward, sending bright streaks of color like a rainbow gone mad, spilling out and over the rhuk's body. The body I'd broken, and now was healing.

Goddesses help us if the bird was lying its face off.

But . . . Balder had not been wrong before, and I trusted him now.

The rainbows flung about us like tiny worms in the air, dancing and tripping over one another as they fell onto the rhuk, burrowing in under the feathers.

The rhuk let out a low breath and . . . stopped moving, the breath in its body stilling. "Shit. Is it dead?"

What if the horn was killing it? I didn't even know if it was male or female. Not that it mattered.

"Excuse me," Reyhan said. "I think someone is coming. I can hear them."

I twisted around to look back the way we'd come. Apparently, our passage and fight with the rhuk had not gone unnoticed. I twisted around and stared out across the desert, not liking what I was seeing. Blocky creatures all in a row and headed straight for us.

I groaned. "Lila, is that . . . what I think those are?"

"Oh man, why can't we catch a break?" she yelped. "Those are pillars, I'm sure of it."

The rock monsters belonging to Asag.

And they'd found us.

The Storm Queen's words rung sharp in his ears.

Kill him.

Tell her you are my son.

Marsum's voice was resigned. *She will want you then. She will overlook the fact that you aren't pure.*

"But I don't want that!" Maks snapped.

The Storm Queen snorted. "Of course you don't want to die. Fool. I know that."

"Not that!"

She crouched beside him and grabbed his chin, forcing him to look up. "Who are you talking to then?"

Marsum slipped forward in a way that Maks didn't think was possible anymore. Maks fought him, but he'd been caught off guard. Marsum spoke, his voice different from Maks's.

"He is my son."

The Storm Queen stumbled back and stood. "Marsum?"

Fuck, shit, damn. He fought to gain control of his own damn body. How the hell did she know Marsum so well? "Yes. I am here, in his head, though he'd much rather I was not. Dani, you want him. He is stronger even than I was."

Dani? That was her name. But by then it was too late, the damage was done in the few seconds it took Maks to gain control once more.

The Storm Queen snapped her fingers. "Take him to my bedchamber. Give him the drug so that he will desire me. I don't care if he is awake. I'll fuck him while he sleeps if I must."

Maks flung himself back against the bonds that held him, but it was no use. "Damn you, Marsum!"

Your death would break Zam. This she can get over. Dani will let you live longer and may even free you if you give her a child.

"You don't know that!" he roared. Because he knew what unfaithfulness had done to Zam's marriage. Steve had cheated on her, lied to her, bedded other women and gotten Kiara *pregnant.*

This . . . Storm Queen . . . was going to put Zam through it all again. With him. Right down to the pregnancy if she could make it happen. He couldn't let it happen.

The hands that carried him out of the room and down the halls were not rough, but he barely saw the ones they were attached to. His mind was caught up in how to set himself free, in how he was going to make it happen.

Because in one way, Marsum was right. He had to survive. Zam wouldn't forgive him for dying either. He had to be smarter than this Dani, this Storm Queen. He let his eyes take in the space, the halls, rather than the thugs that carried him back to the bedroom he knew better than he could have wished.

As quickly as they'd been there, those same hands were just as suddenly gone. He blinked and time seemed to have passed without him registering it.

Was it the last of the other potion?

Was it something else? Because it felt as though he were not truly there. Or maybe this was just some form of shock.

Trauma, his mind whispered. He was dealing with a traumatic experience and his mind was shutting down. In all that he'd faced, in all his life nothing came close to this—this total and complete lack of control, with one exception. When he'd shared his body with the souls of the Jinn masters. But even then . . . it hadn't felt like this.

He blinked and the old woman was there again. Her hair all fluffed up; her eyes as sharp as ever. "Fought off one potion, but she doesn't need you to like her now. She wanted a little loving in her bed, but she'll take you for a good old-fashioned flouncing I suppose if it gives her the beasty child she wants."

The old woman shuffled closer, with a tiny blue tablet just visible in her palm. His hands were tied down, stretched out above his head, and he fought to bring them over his mouth. She cooed and laughed and slipped the blue pill past his lips, then pinched his nose.

He glared up at her.

She smiled. "You think you won? Foolish man. See how you like this."

Reaching to the side table, she picked up a cup of water and poured it on his face so as he opened his mouth to breathe, he had no choice but to take in the water and the pill.

Gagging and choking, he swallowed over and over again, his instincts to live and breathe taking over anything else.

The old woman patted his cheek again. "Don't fret, pretty boy. It'll be over in a jiffy. Just close your eyes and enjoy the ride. Once a day for the next month should do the trick."

He stared at her as the horror truly set in.

This was happening.

He had no choice in this and no choice in how his body responded to whatever it was she'd just given him.

Even as he thought about it, his body was reacting to the little blue pill she'd forced into him. Panic was not something he often gave into, but it crashed over him like a wave from the ocean outside as he hardened.

"Fuck!" He kicked out and rolled as the sheet slipped down his bare body.

"Oh, don't be making me tie your legs down too!" the old woman snapped, a lash coming down across his bare thighs. When had his clothes been stripped off him? Wait, they'd been taken when he'd still thought that Dani was Zam.

He blinked and the Storm Queen strode toward him, naked but for the long silk robe that hung from her shoulders and a clear bottle of liquid in one hand.

"Is he prepped?"

"Of course." The old woman bowed and pointed at his erection as she let herself out.

The Storm Queen made her way to the bed and trailed her fingers up his leg and settled on his hip. "Pity. I was hoping you'd prefer to make this enjoyable." She poured the bottle of liquid over him, warm and greasy.

He bared his teeth at her and let out a low snarl. "I'm going to make you work for this, Dani. I won't go easy for you."

She laughed. "And how is that?"

His snarl turned into a hard smile as he pulled his body through a shift so that he stood in the shackles on four legs as a caracal. Ears pinned, he snarled at her.

Rage flickered across her face. "You think you win because you are a beast? I will force you back!"

He snapped his teeth as he leapt at her, slamming his feet into her chest and throwing her backward. Her eyes went wide as she lost her balance, then hit the far wall hard enough that the wind was knocked out of her, if her gaping mouth was any indication.

She didn't know Jinn like he did. They never expected a physical attack. They were magic, magic all the way.

There was only one option now and he prayed to the desert gods he was making the right choice.

He raced toward the open window as she drew a breath and began to screech for her guards.

How far down would the fall be?

Would he survive? No, he had to.

He pushed off the floor and leapt, his narrow body sliding through the slit, straight out into open air above a raging ocean.

There was a moment of sheer relief, of flight where his body was weightless, and he felt as though he were free.

Maks looked down between his front legs.

The ocean was there, but he was still over the jagged rocks as he began his free fall.

He couldn't tell if he'd make the edge of the water or not, if it would be deep enough. Maybe he'd slide between the rocks.

Nope.

He missed the water.

Crashed into the rocks below, his body snapping in a hundred places at once.

The pain was an explosion inside of him, nerve endings lighting up, and the darkness rolling over him.

Dead, he was dead.

Only . . ..

"Jaysus christos on a spitting camel. Don't tell me *this* is her mate?" The voice was gravelly, male, deep. Maks blinked and stared up at a dark shrouded figure, the hint of horns sticking out from under a cloak and hood as flames licked up around his legs.

He'd have scrambled back only he couldn't move. He looked around, could hear the ocean crashing and there was even a sensation of water against his fur, but he was dead. Or at least he was pretty sure he was dead.

"Quite the pair, aren't they?" a softer, feminine voice said. "I mean, in some ways they are rather amusing, bumbling about trying to save the world from Asag. That they even continue to try is worth something, don't you think?"

Maks managed to blink and pull the woman into view. Soft curves. Long hair that floated like a halo around her body and the brightest blue eyes he'd ever seen.

"What do we do about it? You know that if he dies then she will lose her fucking marbles. She'll kill the Storm Queen, and we still need her. There are only so many who can take on Asag."

"Zam?" He whispered her name.

They both looked at him. If he'd have been able to

move, he'd have squirmed under the energy that flowed around them and *into* him.

"How many times are we to save them?" the male asked, obviously irritated if the wrinkle in his lips was any indication. "I want Asag dead as badly as you, but we are running out of chances here."

"This is the last time . . ." the female said softly. "I have nothing else to give, and neither do you. And yet, despite all this, they are still our best bet. Zamira is still the one that must go on."

"No," Maks whispered. "No, if . . . if you have only one last chance to save one of us." He didn't fully understand the why or wherefore of this place, or the rules, but he did know one thing. "Save her. Save Zam."

The woman crouched next to him and brushed a hand over his face, stroking his ears back to his head. "We are. By saving you, we are saving her. But there are no more chances, and I see all too much ahead of you to believe that you both will survive. A realm of demons is no small task, it is no small place to find yourself. And that is if you both survive the Kingdom of Storms, young Jinn."

He struggled to breathe, his body shutting down so much that even like this, in a corporeal form he knew he didn't have long. He wanted to argue with them, to tell them to let him go and save whatever strange power they had over death to keep Zam alive.

Their hands gripped him at the same time, power rushing through his body like a heat wave off the desert sands, tearing into him. He gasped, choked on a lungful of seawater and then was scrambling up, wobbling on four legs.

A scream of rage ripped through the air above him and he knew his time was limited before Dani saw him and finished what his leap of faith had started.

Forcing his body forward, he dove for a rock, and then another and another until he was under the lip of an overhang. The water was only a few feet below him, the waves splashing up onto his toes where he sat.

He was free of the Storm Queen, sort of, but he had to find a way back to the mainland and off this rock of an island.

"You will not leave here alive!"

Dani's words boomed through the air, punctuated with a bright flash of lightning.

Huddling, he curled up around himself, tucking as far back into the overhang as he could as the ocean below him began to froth and thrash as though the Storm Queen's temper tantrum was feeding it. And maybe it was.

The skies darkened and the wind whipped up, adding to the spray of salty water.

Maks curled tighter around his lithe body and closed his eyes. He just had to wait this out. And when the Storm Queen's power faded, then he'd swim for it.

Through the shark- and monster-infested waters, if the fins and humping bodies through the waves were any indication. A long tentacle reached up the sides of the castle, suction cups popping loud even over the waves. What a shit show he'd been stuffed into.

If he made a swim for it, he'd be in perfect view of any rhuk that might be flying, or guards that might be looking out over the water with long-range weapons.

"Don't go borrowing trouble," he said softly.

He did not expect an answer.

You don't need to, it comes your way as surely as it comes to her, Marsum said with more than a little exasperation in his voice.

Maks pinned his ears to his head and bared his teeth. Even with his eyes closed he could 'see' Marsum. His father sat next to him in his mind's eye.

"Why would you tell her I was your son?"

"Because she was going to kill you, fool," Marsum said, as calm as a summer's day. "You need to live, to survive so you can escape whatever it is comes your way. Didn't I teach you that? You think your body and the usage of it is the worst thing? Idiot."

Maks tried to push his father out of his head, but whatever connection they had seemed to be getting stronger, not weaker. "Go away."

"Can't. Though I can't say I'm not surprised. I thought we were at quits too. Apparently, I am still here, and you are blessed to have me."

Maks was quiet a moment. "What do you know about a pair of demons, one female and beautiful, one male and hideous?"

Marsum sighed long and low. "You met Soleil and

Nico? Well shit, you are in deeper than . . . at least they didn't meet Zam. If they get their hooks into her, then . . ."

Maks groaned and slowly told Marsum what he'd learned when Soleil and Nico had saved his life, healed his broken bones and brought him back to life.

By the end, he was wishing that they had let him die.

The rock monsters—or pillars as we'd learned they were called—were massive, made of rock, and as far as I could tell were pretty much indestructible. Even when I'd used Lilith on them the first time I'd run into them, it had been an effort to harm them. They weren't really alive, so how did you kill them?

Short answer, you didn't. You could slow them down if you were lucky and that was about it.

Vahab peered out into the desert. "What kind of a monster is named a pillar? That's not very awe-inspiring. Are we really running away from it?"

Beside me the massive rhuk pulled itself around so that it was crouched like nothing more than an enormous chicken if I ignored the teeth hanging out over the beak. Dark eyes swept over us. I couldn't help it; I took a step back.

"Look, we've got enough trouble, so you just get out of here." I waved the unicorn horn at the bird before I thought better of it.

The rhuk tipped its head sideways and shuffled into my line of sight. "I can get you to safety. I owe you my life and my freedom. It is the least I can do."

I held a hand up, stopping the big bird. "Listen—"

"Cassandra," she said.

"Cassandra, listen, don't think it's because I don't trust you, because let's be brutally honest, I don't. But letting you wrap your talons around us and fly away to wherever the fuck you want is not a great idea, even on a good day." I pointed at the bodies of the rock monsters rapidly approaching. "Today? Today is not a good day. Get out of here!"

I stuffed the unicorn horn away, leapt on Balder and spun him to blitz into a run as the rhuk launched herself up into the air, wings beating hard and turning up an immediate dust storm. Her body cut the light off from the sun and we stood in her shadow for a second too long.

Behind us Dancer whinnied and as I turned to look, she reared up, but the rhuk already reached for her.

"Damn it, no!" I yelped as I spun Balder around the other way. Reyhan cried out, a hand reaching for her horse.

Dancer fought and wiggled, Vahab did nothing. Fen also did nothing as he wrapped himself tighter around Vahab's neck.

"Fight, damn it!" I yelled at them as I urged Balder to get moving.

"No, this is fine!" Vahab said. "Really, a flight with a rhuk is a wonderful experience! I mean, as long as she doesn't want to eat us."

"Goddess damn it!" We were going to lose Dancer, but we'd also get rid of Vahab and Fen. "I'm sorry, Reyhan."

She cried in my arms as I gave Balder my heels, and I urged him forward. I didn't want to lose Dancer, but there was nothing I could do.

My horse didn't move. He didn't budge as I kissed at him, as I bumped him with my heels. I resorted to flapping my reins, a move that every beginner rider tries once. And like everything else, it did nothing.

"Balder? Come on, friend, let's go!"

He gave a snort and pawed at the ground, but otherwise stood still. Resignation flowed over me as Cassandra's talons wrapped around us. I closed my eyes. It would be just like the dragons carrying us around.

Right?

Not so much. The wingbeats were longer, as if she didn't have as much lift as a dragon, which was strange considering she was all feathers and dragons were giant, heavily muscled lizards. There was a moment I thought she wouldn't be able to get us far enough above the rock monsters.

I clutched Reyhan tight, and Lila clutched me, her claws digging into my scalp and ear.

One beat of the wings, two, three. The pillars were fifty feet away now. I'd have almost preferred if Fen had been carrying us. Despite his attitude, I didn't hate him.

I held my breath as we slowly rose into the air as the first of the pillars swarmed over the last small hill where we'd landed after the cliffside disaster.

One of them was close enough that I could see the orange reflection in its eyes. So, I flipped it off, full well knowing it was Asag staring at me.

The rhuk turned us and flew hard to the northeast. I smacked the piece of bird leg closest to me. "No, we have to go south!"

"It is not safe. I will take you to my true master. He will help."

Oh, for fuck's sake. "No! We have to get to the Storm Queen!"

"Yes, Pazuzu will know what to do next." Her wings didn't falter as we flew away from Maks, away from the Storm Queen. She ignored me completely.

My heart faltered and I fought the tears, gave up and let them fall. Each second that we were apart I could feel our bond breaking a little more. Or maybe it was just my deep-down fear that he would fall into her bed willingly, like Steve had. That I would lose Maks to another woman.

We might be safe from Asag's beasts, but whatever strides we'd taken toward Maks . . . they were gone. What if he wasn't safe? What would the Storm Queen do to him if he fought her attentions? Because despite my fears, the reality was, I knew him heart and soul. He *would* fight her, and he would try to keep himself away from her with all he had. Even if it cost him his life. He was no Steve.

He was no pretend alpha. He was the real deal, knowing when to fight, and when to run.

The fear of him cheating faded and the fear of him dying spiked.

"Why are you crying?" Vahab shouted across at me. "This is wonderful! I haven't seen Pazuzu in years! What a reunion it will be! Ah, he will be so surprised!"

"You will not tell him who you are!" I snapped. "You will keep your damn mouth shut!"

Vahab frowned at me from between the talons of Cassandra the rhuk.

"Why?"

"Because goddess only knows if he hates you too!" I wiped a hand across my face, digging into the anger at Vahab.

Reyhan reached up and touched my face. "Don't cry."

I smiled down at her, feeling the edges of it wobble. "Sorry, kid."

"We're safe now, aren't we?" she whispered as she turned her face into me, snuggling close. I looped an arm around her tiny body.

And I lied to her, the way my parents had lied to me. "Yes, we're safe now. You rest if you can."

A lie, but one that I could hope would turn out more like a truth.

* * *

HOURS OF FLYING over the last of the desert and into the mountains had my anxiety riding so high that if someone had lit a match near me, I was sure I'd explode.

Pazuzu was the next step to get officially closer to Asag. But Maks was the other way.

With the Storm Queen.

"Balder, I hope you are right about this." I kept a hand on his neck. From my shoulder, Lila snorted.

"This is a terrible idea, and I don't approve at all. Do you realize you are so wound up that we haven't even tried to stump each other with Will?" She tugged on my earlobe and then put her head gently against mine, pressing against my temple. "And yes, I am worried about Toad too. He is not very good at staying alive on his own."

"What kind of a name for a man is Toad?" Vahab shouted across from his perch. "Really, that's a shame. Is he ugly? Because if he's ugly I think he will never find himself a woman."

I glared at him, remembering what Lilith had said

about keeping Vahab happy. While I'd yet to see him perform a lick of magic, I had no doubt there was something kicking around in him. "You know, for a powerful Jinn, you surely are the most useless one I've ever met. Not an ounce of magic other than a bit of a smoke show and an attempt at intimidation."

He shrugged and spread his hands wide, his eyes sparkling as we flew. "You know, I find it fascinating that you think the most dangerous Jinn is also the most powerful. I've never found that to be the case. Take you, for example. Not even a flicker of magic in you that I can see, and yet you have a demon chasing you across a desert as if you are the most dangerous thing to him. Isn't that interesting to you?"

It was not. I looked away from him as Cassandra let out a scream that cut the air and made the hair stand up along my body with a rush of pure adrenaline.

"There, ahead!" Lila pointed. I faced forward and sucked in a sharp breath at the sight before me.

Clouds swept away from the top of a mountain, centered between two other mountain tops to reveal a castle set front and center.

Blue stone blocks made up the entirety of it, glittering as though cast through with stars. Spire after spire rose up through a few remaining clouds, each tip of the spire topped with a crystal sun, the rays pointing out in every direction.

"I'm counting over fifty spires," Lila breathed. "That's even bigger than the Ice Witch's castle."

"Yes," I said. "And no easy way for us to get away unless we can convince Fen to carry us?"

I looked across at Vahab and Fen, and the sinewy dragon shook his head. "I cannot carry large loads. My frame is not built for it."

If we landed on that mountain top, in what was apparently Pazuzu's home, we had no way to escape.

In other words, we were about to be royally and completely fucked.

"Cassandra, we don't want to land here!" I yelled up at the rhuk, her wings spread wide enough to block out the sun. Pazuzu's home was getting closer and closer, the blue stone stunning in its beauty and also terrifying in that I could see there was no way out. And while there was no 'good' place to land in the middle of a mountain range, the tippy top of a giant fucking mountain was probably the worst of all the bad options. Especially with horses on board and no way to get them down the goddess-cursed mountain if we needed to make a run for it.

"It is where we are going," she yelled back at me, ducking her head down so she could give me a solid stare out of one dark eye. "You will thank me later. Trust me."

"Oh, I doubt that," Lila muttered. "If I could size up, I could take us away!"

I reached up and put a hand against her side. "I know, my friend, I know."

And I did. Because I felt the limitations that were placed on us, how hard it was to do what we needed to do. And the frustration was massive.

The sweeping castle seemed to open up as we flew closer. Check that, the castle *did* open. The massive, glittering blue stone that made up the structure shifted, chunks grinding as they moved to accommodate the large bird carrying two horses and riders, creating a perfect landing pad.

Cassandra slowed her wingbeats and tried to drop us carefully, but the horses were ready. Both Balder and Dancer surged forward, jumping out of her talons the moment she released them. We skittered across the blue stone courtyard, trotting a few steps before turning around.

Reyhan curled in tighter to me. "I don't think I like this place. It's cold."

She wasn't wrong. The bite of the mountains was sharper here in the courtyard and our clothing was not made for the wintry cold. Weird that we hadn't felt the cold while flying? Or perhaps that was just the adrenaline?

Balder snorted and shook his head, his hooves clattering on the stone. I patted him on the neck. "Oh sure, now you get antsy. A little late, my friend, to change your mind."

Lila slid down the back of my cloak and hid under

the hood, shivering. I took note that Fen did the same thing with Vahab. "Lila. See if you can slip away, unseen," I whispered. "Take Fen and see what you can see."

"Stealth mission," she whispered as she slid down my back and out from under my cloak. "I am on it."

I didn't look for her, but did see Fen suddenly slide down Vahab's back and away to the left. From the corner of my eye, the two tiny dragons climbed the blue stone and slid in through a narrow window.

"Be careful," I whispered to my sister friend, even though she couldn't hear me.

The rhuk settled in behind us, sighing heavily. "I am spent. I must rest."

In other words, we weren't going anywhere, anytime soon.

I didn't dismount Balder. Not even when a portion of the stone in front of us slid left and right, revealing an opening out from which our host stepped.

He looked the same as when I'd seen him in the dream world with Mamitu. Dark hair and eyes, a deep sun-kissed skin and an edge to him that screamed of danger and magic.

He wore a midnight blue outfit, form-fitting pants, tunic and cloak that hung from his shoulders. Like the blue stone, there was a glitter in the material that seemed to me to be a spattering of stars.

"I like his shirt," Reyhan said.

I held her a little tighter, but spoke to Pazuzu. "Your bird brought us here, Pazuzu."

Ignoring us, he strode across the open space to Cassandra, holding his hands up to her. She bowed her head, placing her closed beak into his cupped hands. "Beautiful, how did you escape the storm bitch?"

For a moment I thought he meant me, and my ire bristled.

"This one freed me from the Storm Queen." Cassandra blinked and rolled her eyes to me, never taking her beak from her master's hands. "I am home."

"You are home. And I am beyond happy to have you here." He kissed her beak and a great fat tear slid from her eyes and down across his fingers.

Only then did he turn to us, tucking his tear-stained hand behind his back.

He gave a half bow from his waist. "You found the Vessel of Vahab." His eyes slid to my companion on my left. "And you brought him with you?"

I shrugged. I should have known he'd recognize the Jinn. "What was I supposed to do with him?"

"Kill him is the answer that most would give." Pazuzu sighed. "But as always, he's found his way out of a rather tight predicament." And then he smiled at Vahab. "How did you like that vase?"

Vahab smiled right back. "Lovely; I felt it rather large for my time there, but I am not one to complain."

I looked at Pazuzu in time to see the skin around his eyes and mouth tighten.

"You two going to fight?" I asked. "I mean, I wouldn't mind seeing Vahab smacked around a bit."

Pazuzu snorted and looked away from Vahab, though it seemed to cost him an effort. "You and many, many others, young Desert Cursed."

My turn to grimace. "I really wish you wouldn't call me that."

"The truth stings, does it not?"

"Like a fucking hornet's nest on my ass," I mumbled.

Pazuzu gave a low chuckle. "Come, let me feed you and give you your next task."

If I hadn't already been sitting I might have fallen over. "No, my mate is—"

"Is trapped with the Storm Queen, yes? Rather a bit of a pickle if you ask me. She does not like to give up the things she believes are hers, such as the rhuk that are born here in the mountains." Pazuzu spun and flipped his cloak out behind him, the stars in the material glittering, drawing my eyes.

They did more than draw Reyhan's eyes. She leapt off Balder's back and ran after the man who'd brought us here before I could grab her.

"Reyhan, no!"

She slid to a stop only when her fingers brushed against the material, sliding it across her hand. "It's pretty."

I dismounted and hurried over to her, taking her hand and pulling her away from Pazuzu. His eyebrows were high. "Cat shifter, is she? They always like the sparkles."

I tugged her so she was a little behind me. "And you use the sparkles to draw them to you? To trap them?"

He shook his head. "No. It is not so devious as that. I just like the flair of them."

I wasn't sure I believed him, but I followed him in through the opening in the stone wall. I mean, we could have stayed on the rooftop, but it was cold. Too cold for us, and too cold for Balder and Dancer. "What about the horses? They can't stand this weather."

"The rhuk will keep them warm," Pazuzu said with a wave of his hand over his head. "Pet. Take them in."

"Of course," she said, and I watched as she spread her wings and dragged the horses in under her. Like a hen with her chicks, which brought a smile to my lips. Balder nickered, and lay down next to her, then poked his head out from under her wing. Dancer followed his lead though her eyes held far more suspicion.

"They will be safe and warm," Pazuzu said. "I will send feed and warm water for them as well." He snapped his fingers and there was movement in the air. The feeling of something brushing past me.

But there was no one there.

"Is it a ghost?" Reyhan whispered. I picked her up quickly and settled her on my back.

"No idea."

Pazuzu kept on, and I followed, noticing that Vahab

had been rather quiet since their back and forth. I glanced over at him.

His face was stonier than I'd seen it in the short time I'd known him. "Didn't get the reception you were hoping for?"

His brows furrowed. "Paz and I were good friends. I do not like believing that he turned on me to save himself. Which is what I take from his comments about the vessel."

Interesting.

"Or maybe you turned on him?" I offered. "I mean, you are a Jinn, after all."

He shot me a look. "What kind of Jinn have you been dealing with?"

"The worst."

And then my words were dry in my mouth because the scene in front of me stole them away. The stones behind us slid closed and the space we stood in lit up.

The glittering sparkles inside the stone now glowed, giving off enough light to see by. The space adjusted, stairs leading down placing themselves in our path so that there was no opportunity to do anything but follow. The lights moved and danced, flickering and drawing the eyes as though we walked amongst the sky and the stars. There was no space ahead or beyond, we just . . . were.

"This is fucking pretty," Reyhan breathed, and I choked.

"We don't use that word, remember?" And I cringed even as I said it. "Or at least you don't."

Reyhan snorted. "You use it all the time."

"Can't argue with that," Vahab said.

With my mouth clamped shut, because no, I couldn't argue it, we descended the long flight of stairs, the moment of feeling as though we floated amongst the stars gone.

The expanse opened up to a ridiculously high ceiling covered with chandeliers of every size and shape, crystal, gold, silver, candelabras.

I blinked as two small dragons slid across the ceiling, clinging with their tiny claws as they inspected things.

I looked away as Fen bit Lila on the tail.

Goddess, she was going to be pissed if he ended up being 'the one'. Which only made me smile.

Perhaps something good would come out of the introduction of Vahab and Fen.

"Welcome. Please sit and rest, eat. Drink." Pazuzu waved his hands wide, and tables appeared in front of us, covered with more food than I'd seen in my entire lifetime.

Reyhan leapt off my back and ran for the closest thing—suckling pig. She tore a leg off and bit into it. While I had a little more restraint, it wasn't much.

Living in the desert, you learned to eat and drink when you could. As worried as I was for Maks, I knew I'd be better served to save him on a full belly. That being refreshed and full was a better way to face a battle.

I moved toward the table and tried to take it all in before I actually scooped something up. Cheeses and fresh breads that still steamed, butter melting through the slices, sweet jams and thick pots of mashed root vegetables, ice cold jugs and steaming jugs full of liquid spices and trouble . . . fresh ice pears, frost grapes and little, tiny things that I wasn't sure what to make of. I picked one up.

"That's a prawn. From the Sea of Storms." Pazuzu sat himself down. "Peel it and eat the flesh. You cats always like the seafood."

Peeling off the shell, I popped the tiny thing in my mouth and had to fight back the moan. After that the food was a blur of tastes and scents that I ate until my belly ached at the edges and I was sure I was going to puke it all up.

"Enough," I whispered, pushing my chair back and grabbing a goblet of steaming wine. Something warm.

Nope, not wine. Mulled tea. Even better. I took a sip and looked across at Pazuzu. "Well played. Now, what is this task you have for me? And why should I take it instead of going for Maks?"

Pazuzu sat across from me. Vahab and Reyhan sat on either side of my chair.

Our host clasped his fingers together and put his mouth to the edge of them. "If you do not take the three tasks the way they are given, you will never be able to face Asag. It is a part of the rules."

"Why not?" I asked, and was surprised when Vahab answered me instead of Pazuzu.

"Because there are rules to demons. That is the one downfall to them. They have rules and if you follow by them and beat them at their own game, then you win, and they are sent back to the realm of demons. That is what was done when Asag was brought here by Soleil and Nico, the first demons." He picked at his teeth with a thin bone.

I stared across at Pazuzu. "You can tell me more than Mamitu?"

"She does not know as much as I in regard to Asag. I have . . . more dealings with him than I'd like and so I have gleaned more information than she." He pulled a face and picked up a goblet, swirling it. "Vahab is correct. If you follow the rules and win the game, then you can send Asag back to the realm of demons. But you must understand too one very important thing."

He lifted his eyes and I lifted my chin. "And what is that?"

"The game is rigged."

10

I grimaced as if my tea had gone sour. "Of course the game is rigged. I mean, that is no surprise to me that Asag rigged this so that he would never lose his hold on this side of the walls."

Pazuzu sighed. "As I said, demons are bound by rules. There must always be a way to send them back to the realm of demons. But once they are here, they will do all they can to make sure any who would seek to remove them face near impossible tasks."

"Near impossible," I said. "But not impossible."

"That is the game," Pazuzu said. "And as such, I give you the next task in front of you."

I clutched the goblet harder and waited for the proverbial bomb to drop. But he hesitated. I finally prompted him. "And? Spit it out, man."

Vahab laughed. "He is no more human than I am."

"Semantics," I threw at him. "What is the task?"

Pazuzu settled back in his chair. "You need to steal an item from the Storm Queen."

A barking laugh rippled out from Lila up on the ceiling, but I wasn't sure anyone else heard it over my own howl of laughter. It took me a few moments to calm myself. Because of all the things they could ask me, stealing an item from a powerful being was right up my alley.

I finally slowed and caught my breath. "What kind of item?"

"A diamond," Pazuzu said. "A very large, yellow diamond, roughly the size of a small melon."

Too easy, this would be too easy, and *that* made my laughter dry up. There had been nothing easy about getting to Vahab, there would be nothing easy about getting to the diamond. I looked over at my Jinn companion to see him swirling his drink as he stared at Pazuzu. His eyes were thoughtful, and him being this quiet made me nervous. My spine twitched as if my tail were available to tick back and forth. "What's so special about this diamond? Does it hold the first demon in it?"

Pazuzu shook his head. "No, this diamond holds the source of all magic. And it is why the Storm Queen remains sovereign in a realm ruled by a demon. She is its protector and draws strength from its proximity. You must steal it from her. And then you must carry it with you through your remaining task until you face Asag."

I blinked. "Oh, is that all? Just the *source of all magic.*

That's not heavy at all. Tell me, if I break it open, you know, accidently break it? What happens then?"

Our host paled. "I do not believe that would go well for anyone. The diamond is a living, breathing creation. We call it a diamond because that is the best way to describe it, not because it is truly a simple gemstone."

Better and better. Sentient items for the win, anyone?

Vahab stood up. "There is no good reason to take that diamond away from her. I placed it in her mother's mother's mother's hands before I was stuffed into the vase. And if that family line has kept it safe all these years, then they should be left alone."

Pazuzu looked at Vahab and rolled his eyes at the Jinn, then turned to me again. "There is no other pathway for you to face Asag. The Beast from the East has not made this easy. The diamond is buried within the heart of the island. That is all I know."

There was a flurry of wings overhead and the two small dragons dropped to the middle of the table. Lila landed in a soup.

Fen landed in a large fruit salad.

"You want to tell her about the prisoners you have locked up?" Lila snapped.

"They are not prisoners." Pazuzu sighed.

"Yeah? They seem to think they are." Lila stalked across the table, kicking stuff off. "And seeing as they are cousins to dragons, I would like to know just what you are doing with them? Or shall I spit acid on your face and see if you'd like to answer me after I've melted your skin off?"

I stood up, wobbled a little, and realized I'd had more than I'd thought to drink. Reyhan was slumped in her chair, head tipped forward and sleeping on the edge of the table. I tried to look quickly over at Vahab, but the quick movement had me reeling. "What . . . ?"

"A light sedative for you all." Pazuzu sighed again. "It is part of the game that Asag has set up. Lucky for you, your dragon friends have not partaken in the food, so they will be able to help you. You must escape my home, and ride to the Kingdom of Storms, retrieve the yellow diamond, and bring it back to me in order to complete this task. Fail, and find death. Succeed and find yourself one step closer to facing Asag."

Vahab shoved to his feet, unsteady but standing. "Damn you, Paz!"

"It is not my idea!" Pazuzu snapped back. "I am as bound as you were in that vase, Vahab. The rules are the rules. It is what we all agreed to in order to live and hope to see enough days that he would be brought down!" His voice was rising rapidly. "If I could kill him myself, I would. But that is not for me. That task comes to her." He thrust a finger at me. "The only one to reach past the first challenge in all these years. And she is . . . she is just a mutt, with no magic, and she reminds me of—"

"Me?" offered Vahab, still shaky, but holding his own. "The one Jinn who stopped Asag in his tracks toward the western desert and confined him to his city which is why he has his little generals no doubt doing his dirty work?"

I did a slow turn to look at Vahab. "How?"

"It's a long story." He waved a hand at me. "But this one, Mamitu and Gorg are the three who turned on me, to save themselves. If they'd stood firm, we could have stopped him. I had him on the ropes."

Pazuzu shook his head. "That was never going to happen. He was going to kill us all, and Mamitu could see it! If we were dead, what then? We convinced him to use you as the first challenge. Of course, we thought you'd be out long before now! We helped all those who came, at costs to ourselves, Vahab. We . . . we did our best."

The sedation in me bubbled up and I groaned as I sagged back to my chair. Lila ran across the table to me as the two men argued back and forth.

"Zam!"

"M'okay," I mumbled. "Juss sleep for bit."

My eyes slammed shut and that was that. I was out cold.

A STREAM of light across my face woke me from the food Pazuzu had so freely fed us. Why did he have to knock us out? What part of the game was that? A stupid one, in my opinion. I rolled to my side with a groan, sluggish with every move as if the sedation was still rumbling through me.

I didn't feel sick, or injured, just . . . tired. I'd been put in a bed that was soft and warm, the blankets heavy around my limbs.

"It's about time!" Lila crawled out from under one of the pillows. "We have to go. I've been poking at your ear and screaming for hours!"

I stretched and yawned wide enough that my jaw cracked, and my spine popped, my head fuzzy. "Where are we?"

"ARE YOU SERIOUS?" Lila flipped around so that we were face to face and she could grab both my ears and shake my head. "We have a deadline that is stupid ridiculous and you're sleeping away the day. I don't care if you're full of sleepy time potion, we need to move!"

I swung my legs off the bed and grabbed at my clean clothes that were hung over the back of a chair. Pants, shirt, boots, cloak, weapons. I blinked at the sword that lay across the chair and the note on it.

"You will need this."

11

M for Mamitu? Damn it all to hell. With a grimace I grabbed the sheath that Lilith sat in and strapped it to my back, over my cloak.

Immediately she spoke.

Do not leave me behind again.

"Don't fucking well try to take over my body then," I growled. My mind was clearing, and the night before came back to me. I could recall bits and pieces of the conversation between Pazuzu and Vahab. They'd argued a long time; the sleeping draught that had taken me and Reyhan out apparently hadn't worked as well on Vahab. Or maybe he hadn't been drugged?

Lila zipped around the room. "We gotta go. Between the ice drakes in the dungeons and the pillars on their way, we have to go."

I had my hand on the door. "Ice drakes? Wait, the pillars are coming?"

Lila landed on my shoulder. "They are here, at the gates of the castle demanding entrance. I'm betting that was the reason for the sedation. To give them time to get here. I hate this Pazuzu shit."

A thump rumbled through the floor, punctuating her words.

"And the ice drakes . . . they are wingless, four-legged dragons that look a bit more like horses. They are savvy through the mountains and rocks. Kind of like goats." She blew out a sigh. "I thought they were captive, but they aren't really. Pazuzu just doesn't let them go far because of Asag."

"You talked to them?"

"Yes, I went back to speak to them while you were out cold." She hunched her shoulders.

"Let's go," I said. "We can't save them, and we need to get to the rooftop." Fingers crossed that Cassandra could get us out of here and back to the desert. That should put some space between us and Asag's monsters.

I looked around the room and a sudden spike of anxiety hit me in the gut. "Where is Reyhan?"

"I don't know," Lila said, her voice pitched with stress.

I almost ripped the door off the hinges as I flung it open. "Reyhan!" Her name echoed through the spacious building, bouncing off the blue stone. Another shudder rippled the stone. "Lila, did you look for her?"

"I sent Fen to look while I kept an eye on you," she said. "He said he couldn't find her anywhere."

I drew a slow breath, scenting the air, but already knowing I'd find her faster on four legs. I stepped through the doorway in my mind that took me from two to four legs and a moment later shook out my black fur.

My smaller shape was about the same size as Lila, and far better for sneaking around than the large jungle cat. "Lila, go to Balder, tell him to be ready. I'll meet you there with her."

"Be careful, Zam. Nothing here is as it seems. It feels . . . off."

I patted her quick with a paw, then raced away, through the hallway, scenting for Reyhan's distinct perfume. Desert and cub, jungle and child. The seconds and then minutes ticked by as I checked rooms, went down stairwells, until finally near the dining hall I caught a whiff of the little girl.

In this form I could pick up the tang of the potion still lingering on the food and drink and I cursed myself for not being smarter. For not being more careful.

Food and drink, they were a weakness. All I had to do was look at the țuică we'd drunk down more than once to know it.

Nose to the ground, I opened my mouth as I drew in the smells across the back of my throat, making sure I was on the right track. Maks was better at this tracking business, and I missed him keenly. Not only for his ability, but for the fact that I knew he was in trouble, and it would be more time than I wanted to get to him.

And I couldn't help but feel the longer we were apart, that it was not going to go well when I found him.

"No," I whispered. "Not right now. Reyhan first. Maks next."

Clearing my mind of my mate, I hurried through the room, picking up the smell of the little girl on the far side, against a wall that looked as though there were no doorway. Yet the scent led right to it. A whoosh of air trickled out from between a thin gap of the wall and the floor.

A screeching groan of stone on stone and then a booming crash shook the walls around me. "Fuck."

A tap on the other side of the wall and a quiet voice whispered, "We don't say that here."

I shifted back to two legs and put my hands against the space. "Reyhan, are you okay?"

"Pazzy said I should stay in here and stay quiet. That the bad man was coming for me." Her voice shook a little.

The bad man . . . Asag? His pillars?

It hit me in the guts. The pillars weren't hunting for me, they weren't chasing me across the desert.

They were chasing Reyhan.

Asag wanted the little girl, and he'd sent his minions after her. I'd just gotten in the way.

The question was, did I leave her hidden, or take her with me?

12

Let's be honest, there was no question. Reyhan was safer with me, I just had to find a way to throw off Asag long enough to give us space.

I looked back at the spread on the table, all the food, right down to the suckling pig that was about the size of a small child. Next to it was a piglet that was smaller yet. My mind raced as I considered my options, and how to pull this off.

Doubt crept in. Could Pazuzu keep her safer than me? Did I dare to leave her here? Was she safer without me?

The strongest Jinn weren't those with the best magic. But those with the most cunning. That was what Vahab had said. And in that moment . . . I believed him.

"Take your clothes off, and shift," I said. "Hurry."

"My clothes go with me." Her voice was muffled. The castle listed and I went to one knee.

"Just do it, Reyhan, I need you to trust me!" I yelled as I scrambled up and ran for the table. A simple double cross would be to take the piglet with me, pretending that I had Reyhan and draw the pillars away.

But if I dressed the large pig in her clothes, leaving behind something of her to draw them, and then took her with me . . . maybe that would buy us more time. And I would not worry myself sick if she were with me.

I snatched up the piglet, shaking the red fruit out of its mouth as I ran back to the hidden door. Sliding my hands over the space, it took me only a moment to find the latch just above my head. One stone a little smaller than the others depressed when I pushed against it.

The stone slid sideways, revealing a beautiful room with a plush bed, a stack of books and simple toys, food and water, even a bathtub. Perfect for a hidden prisoner. Reyhan sat on the bed in her jungle cat form, green eyes watching me close.

I scooped up her discarded clothes and yanked them onto the body of the pig, then stuffed it into the bed, pulling the covers up to its chin.

Reyhan pawed at a leather bag on the bed that had two shoulder straps. "Smart girl!" I scooped it up, popped her in it and slung it onto my back, flipping my cloak over it and hiding her even better. Her tiny claws dug into the back of my one shoulder as she peered out. "Stay down for now."

I blew out all but one candle in the room and

turned and ran, hitting the button that closed the door as we slipped through. The stairs we'd entered Pazuzu's castle in led us up and up and up as the boom of the structure being blown apart below us sent shards of dust flying around us and bits of ice.

At the top of the stairs, I paused and looked out on a scene that stole my breath away.

Cassandra, Balder and Dancer were on one side of the rooftop, and between them and me was a dozen of the rock monsters. Lila zipped back to me as Vahab stumbled into my back.

"What have we here? Oh, that's not good. Looking for the girl, are they?" Vahab sighed and put a hand right on the backpack. Right on Reyhan. "They will have to tear the castle apart before they find her."

"Cassandra, fly the horses out of here!" I yelled.

Balder reared up, and struck out at one of the pillars, but barely dented him. This was bad. This was so bad. I spun as Cassandra lifted off and reached for the two horses. I could do nothing else for them as I ran back into the castle. We had to find another way out of here.

"Lila!" I yelled for her and she was there in a flash, flying alongside me as I ran down the stairs. The rumbling of heavy feet behind me told me that we were not going to be allowed to just make a run for it without pursuit.

But it's what we had and so I would find a way to make it work for us.

A stone flung by my head, ruffling my hair. It bounced off the wall ahead of me, shattered and sent shards everywhere.

My face and neck got sliced, Vahab yelped like a kicked puppy and we kept on running.

"Where the hell is Pazuzu?"

"Hiding, most likely," Vahab said. "He's a coward. I see that more clearly now."

I leapt through a doorway that thankfully led downward. "Lila. Think the ice drakes would take us for a ride to get down the mountain?"

"If it meant their freedom, yes," she said.

She shot out in front of me and led us along. I didn't ask where Fen was.

Lila did. "Where is he?" She suddenly turned on Vahab and he shrugged.

"He was snooping the last I checked near Pazuzu's quarters."

Lila's face tightened. "Two more lefts and a set of stairs takes you to the drakes. I'll get Fen. Idiot."

Before I could argue with her, she was gone. Literally in a flash, gone.

"They are going to be cute together," Vahab said. Another time I would have laughed. But I was saving my breath. Even if I agreed with him. They would make a cute pair.

The next two lefts I took at top speed as rocks and stones flung toward us, sending slices through clothing and skin.

One more turn and the stairs appeared. I leapt forward, letting the freefall momentum take me more than halfway down before I landed with a stumble and kept on running.

Vahab was well behind me, but he had his Jinn magic should he decide to use it. I wasn't saving him again.

At the bottom of the stairs was a large iron door. I grabbed the handle and shoved it sideways, the gears grinding slowly.

"Hurry your ass up!" I yelled at Vahab. The pillars were right behind him and as he slid through the doorway, an arm shot through. I was sliding the door back on it, pinning it in place.

"Vahab!"

"Nothing I can do." He didn't even help me hold the door.

I had to keep them there a minute longer. The door squealed. "We have to keep them from the secret room! We need to keep them here as long as we can!" I yelped and glared at Vahab who gave me a smile and touched his nose.

"They won't find her, the room is too well hidden!" he shouted back, grinning even though his tone was one of smug confidence. At least he followed my lead. And maybe it would work . . . .

The arm pulled back and I slammed the door closed.

"They'll be back," Vahab said. "Maybe not for

hours, but they'll be back."

I stared past him at the creatures crowding forward, noses outstretched.

About the size of a horse, maybe a little bigger, they walked on four legs with a leaner body than Lila had, though not snake-like as Fen was. More . . . well, more horse-like. No wings, but they had long loose scales that ran down their necks, and the tails were unreal—long, like whips with barbs on the end. Between their bodies and their legs were thin membranes of skin that glittered translucent. Pale, they were shades of white, gray and light blue. They'd disappear in the mountains and the snow.

I stared at the one who drew closest. "Ice drake? My friend Lila said you were here."

The long muzzle bared longer teeth at me. "Who are you?" Female, this was a female by the pitch of her voice.

"Look." I shifted the bag on my back, feeling Reyhan settle down and begin to purr. "We need a way out of here, and you want to escape, right?"

She ignored my question as she tipped her head to the side and her loose neck scales flared up, like a cat puffing herself to look bigger. "What are you?"

"Jinn." Vahab touched his chest. "That one is a half-breed Jinn."

"Don't you want to get out of here?" I repeated my question. "Or are you trapped?"

Her nostrils flared and her tongue flicked out, ice

droplets falling from it. "We could leave if we wanted to."

"Well, the castle is coming down around us, so you might want to do that," Vahab said. "We just want to hitch a ride."

"Why would we do that?"

I looked around the pens. Comfortable, they were being treated well by all accounts with the cleanliness and the food and bedding. "Because I think if you could have left by now you would have."

The castle shook and listed again, throwing us all to one side. I held up my hands. "Look, I am trying to stop Asag. I need to get to the desert edge where my horse will be waiting—"

The ice drake leapt forward and shoved her face against mine. "You would face down the Beast from the East? You think you can kill him?"

Her blueish white scales drew my eyes like crystal, but it was her violet eyes, so like Lila's, that I couldn't escape. "I have to. There is no choice now." And as the words left my mouth, I knew that they were truth. There was no choice. I was on a runaway horse headed straight for a demon that everyone was terrified of.

Whether I liked it or not.

The ice drake tipped her head to the side. "We will carry you down the mountain. For a price."

Vahab snorted. "You don't have room to negotiate. You're trapped here, and we are freeing you. You should just say thank you."

Said the Jinn who'd been trapped and said he wanted to negotiate his freedom with extra perks. Even if he'd been lying, the irony was still there.

The lead female wrinkled her lips up over her mouthful of teeth. "Good luck then, escaping down a mountain that is unscalable for any who do not have wings, or ride an ice drake."

I shoved Vahab to the side. "He's not in charge here."

"Good, I was worried for you that a stupid man like that might be running your life." The ice drake eyed me up. "What is your offer?"

"The three of us taken down the mountain and to the desert edge where my horses wait," I took a breath, "you gain your freedom. I have a better chance at—"

The castle listed hard, and we were all thrown to the right, slammed into the blue stone walls.

"Get on, we will discuss when we are free!" the ice drake shouted. I didn't wait for another offer. I ran to her side and leapt up onto her back. Whatever the cost she would demand, I would pay it. Because there really was no choice.

She turned, rolling back on her haunches and spinning hard to the left, almost losing me in that first quick move. I grabbed hold of her as best I could, squeezing her with my legs and gripping the long, soft scales that fluttered down her neck.

The leader of the ice drakes leapt forward, straight

toward a wall that dissolved as her nose touched it. "See, we could leave."

Something wasn't adding up here. I didn't know what yet, but I had a feeling we'd find out soon enough.

Yup, soon enough came rather quick.

13

The female ice drake I was riding leapt out of the castle as the stones began to crumble down, the entire structure imploding on itself.

"Lila!" I yelled her name, hoping she would hear me. She would get out; I was sure of it. A shiver wracked me as the cold of the mountains slid through my thin clothes.

I blinked, realizing we weren't running straight downhill. Not really. The membranes under the ice drake's legs had caught the wind and we were kind of floating and falling at the same time. Here and there the ice drakes hit the ground, a chunk of rock, a lump of snow, and bounced back up again as they let gravity take over.

"This is lovely!" Vahab yelled across at me as his

hair kind of floated up around his head. He looked mad, as if he were in some sort of psychedelic dream.

I clung harder to the ice drake and said nothing.

It was not lost on me that the ice drake had perked up when Vahab had said he was a Jinn, and that I was half-Jinn.

What were the ice drakes doing, staying with Pazuzu if they hadn't wanted to be there?

A screech cut through the air, that turned into a snarling growl. We were in between floating bounds and the ice drake below me tensed.

"That is the price," she shouted. "Kill the Ijiraq. The shapeshifter with a thousand shapes, and all the malevolence of a demon! They nearly wiped our herds out."

"Oh, is that all?" I muttered as I twisted around but could see nothing. "Where is it?" Wouldn't a creature like that be large enough to take on the ice drakes? I couldn't imagine it staying small.

"You cannot see it straight on, you can only see it from the corner of your eye!" she said. "They were created by Jinn, so you can rid us of them!"

I looked across at Vahab. "This is on you! Get rid of it!"

He held up both hands, palms up. "I cannot."

"WHY NOT?" both I and the ice drake yelled at the same time. A shimmer to my left, right in the corner of my eye stilled me.

The body was that of a huge man, thin and wiry, covered in no fur even in this cold weather. Symbols I couldn't quite read were etched across his narrow, bony chest. His eyes flashed red right before he tipped his head back and let out that screeching roar that cut through everything.

"Kill it, Vahab!" I said. "Don't tell me you can't! You're the first Jinn, the most powerful Jinn!" Maybe appealing to his ego would do the trick. Or maybe not.

Vahab shrugged. He fucking *shrugged*. "Do you think that Asag let me keep my powers, any more than he let you keep yours?"

"Go as fast as you can!" I yelled at the ice drake.

"I am, but it is not just the Ijiraq!" She tipped her head to the right.

A howl of another creature spun through the air and I twisted to the other side to see a lumbering, massive bear-like creature with deep blue fur. It ran on four legs that were wide and splayed for the snow, and had a three-pronged tail with hooks in the end of it.

And it was, of course, coming straight for us. I scrambled for my hip and the few weapons I had, one of which was a grenade set for my shotgun. I yanked the pin on one, and threw the seemingly harmless ball at the oncoming beast.

"Flatten!" I yelled. I had no idea if they could slow our downward trajectory, but it was worth trying.

The herd of ice drakes tucked their legs in tight and instead of floating down the mountain we were suddenly full on falling.

We hit the snowpack and sunk under the first layers of it as the grenade went off.

The concussion rippled through us, throwing us all sideways even under the snow. Like being in the water, I tumbled away from the ice drake, losing her in the chaos. Reyhan gave a screech, but she was still in her bag on my back.

As the world calmed, I pulled myself up out of the snow. No longer white, it was flecked with the blood and guts of the bear. But where was the Ijiraq? I scanned the area as ice drakes popped up from the snow and shook themselves clean. I kept looking from the corner of my eye as my body tensed, feeling the beast near even though I couldn't see it.

I can help.

Lilith's whisper was right there, and I reached for the handle, stopping just shy of it. "I don't think so."

Instead, I pulled two short daggers that I always kept for backup. They would have to do.

"You cannot kill it with mortal weapons!" the female ice drake said. "It is magic or nothing."

"Nothing it is then!" I said, and then I paused as a thought hit me. When I'd had the flail and shifted while I carried it, the weapon had made me stronger but wasn't able to take over. Would it be the same with Lilith?

I shrugged out of the backpack holding Reyhan as Lila swept into view. I tossed her the kid. "I'm going to try something."

"Not even a hello? How are you? What the hell happened? I mean, let's be honest, I found you nice and easy, only you would think it a good idea to toss a grenade on the side of a freaking mountain! Do you know that you're triggering a landslide? And it's coming fast?" Her words tumbled over and over at a speed I could barely keep up with.

"I love you too, glad you're safe, now I have to kill something." I blew a breath out and shifted into my jungle cat form. I'd held Lilith before when I'd shifted, but I'd not noticed any extra power or strength. That being said, she'd been quieter then.

I closed my eyes and drew in a breath. The Ijiraq was to my left. I spun, eyes open but not looking at it. There it was in the corner of my vision, reaching for one of the ice drakes that was struggling out of the snow. I leapt sideways and tackled it to the ground, and the fucker disappeared from under me.

"Side of your eyes, Lila, can you help me spot it?"

"I can," Fen answered as he landed on my back, his claws and long tail tightening around me.

Good enough. I would take his help.

"Left," he yelped and I spun, swiping with my claws as fast as I could without looking. The Ijiraq screeched as I caught a leg, and dug in deep to the flesh and tendons.

But before I could get a second blow, I looked too close at it, and the beast was gone again.

"It's bleeding!" Lila yelled. "I see blood on the snow

now even though I can't see the body or wounds! Hurry, the snow is coming down faster!"

That had to be good—except for the avalanche, of course. "Come on then!" I snarled and let out a roar of my own.

The ground around us rumbled and I took a step back.

Everything happened too fast for me to stop. That step back took me to the edge of a cliff I didn't see. The Ijiraq tackled me, and we went over in a burst of snow, blood and teeth as the avalanche I'd triggered slammed into us. I closed my eyes and clawed and bit at the beast, feeling my way to its belly as we fell. If it was the last thing I did, I would kill it. Screeching, the Ijiraq clawed and bit back, but I wasn't about to back down now.

I was going to regret this, maybe I'd hit the rocks at the bottom, maybe I'd die for real this time.

I didn't know.

I almost didn't care and as I felt that sensation of apathy, I knew that Lilith still had some hold of me in this shape too.

Our freefall stopped suddenly, and the Ijiraq let go of me, pushed away.

Or maybe torn away was a better word for it. I peeked with one eye, already knowing what had happened. The feel of a dragon's talon was something very specific, and I peered up at Fen as he undulated above me. He'd shifted to his larger form to save me.

"Do not get used to it," he grumbled.

I bared my teeth in a cat grin. "Thanks."

We waited as the avalanche continued past us, the ice drakes navigating it as if it were flat, not undulating ground.

A shiver coursed through me, dancing along my limbs and making them shake like I'd touched something electrical.

Only a few heartbeats passed before the snow was done with its freefall. Fen set me down where the ice drakes waited and then he flung what remained of the Ijiraq out into open air. I could see it now, clearly. Limbs limp, fur no longer taking any sort of shape other than what it was in that moment.

"Is it dead?"

"Yes." The female ice drake came up to us. "That one is dead. Your strength, half-Jinn, has saved us."

I shifted back to two legs, my wounds healing as they did when I went between shifts. Grimacing, I wobbled and reached out to her for balance. Lila landed on her back. "Zam?"

"The Ijiraq's bite is terrible," the ice drake said. "She will need to rest."

Need to rest? The words tumbled through me. "Can't. We have to go. Meet Balder." Even as I spoke my strength fled, my breath came in gasps and I fought to stay upright.

Arms tucked around me, and I was lifted up onto the back of a dragon. I rolled my head to see Vahab smiling down at me, and his hand slid up *way* too far on my ribs.

"Fen and I will take her."

"Mother fucker . . ." I managed as Lilith raged on my back.

How dare he touch you like that?

I didn't disagree but my body was too busy fighting off whatever mojo the damn Ijiraq had shoved into me.

"What the actual fu—" Lila yelled as I was manhandled—in the most literal of sense.

"Fen," I whispered the dragon's name and he sighed.

"I can't stop him, Zam. I'm sorry."

So that said a lot about their relationship. "Where are you taking me?" That's what I wanted to ask, what I got out was 'where'.

"Anywhere I wish," Vahab stroked a hand over my head. "I've been alone a long time. I'm looking forward to this."

He . . . did he really mean to think he'd *take* me like this?

I closed my eyes. Not because I'd given up, not by a long shot. But because I would need my strength when I cut his balls off and fed them to Lila.

He stayed in that cave against the edge of the sea for a full day while the Storm Queen and her cronies searched the water for his body. Or he assumed that was what they were searching for. Goddess only knew what she'd do if she got a hold of a body where she thought the balls were still somehow usable.

A shudder rippled down his spine and he tucked himself deeper into the tight crevice that he'd found. The rocks dug into him on all sides, but that was better than being out in the open where he could be picked off.

Marsum sat beside him, incorporeal but there. Or maybe it was just his mind breaking and so he called up the one person he knew would never truly let him be.

"All this water, and not a drop to drink," Marsum said. "What will you do when your thirst drives you out?"

The question was valid. But Maks had no answer for it. "Tell me again about Soleil and Nico."

Marsum sighed. "They are the first demons, created . . . or come into existence, however it happened. And they have always and forever wanted this world to be home to their children. If they save you, then you are bound to them in a way that you cannot break until you return a favor that they see fit."

"Even though I asked them not to."

"That is the nature of those two. They don't have to be asked. They can give a boon and call in on it later. Asag was a favorite of theirs." Marsum's voice flickered as did his body. "They want him to rule. I just can't understand why they would save you? I mean . . . unless there is something in you that they want too?"

Maks was hoping that perhaps, perhaps this was just a terrible fever dream as he lay dying on the rocks. A figment of his imagination that would never come to fruition.

Beyond that, there was one thing he knew he had to do. He had to get back into the castle. It was the only place where there would be water and food, and more places to hide.

The sun had dipped below the edge of the horizon and the water and rock around him grew dark.

With the clouds above blocking out the light from any stars or the moon, it would be the best chance he had at sneaking back into the Storm Queen's castle. "Did you know her well?" he asked Marsum before he could catch the question and swallow it down.

"We corresponded some," Marsum said. But nothing more.

Maks tipped his head and one ear toward what he was now considering a figment of his imagination. "Am I related to her?"

"Gods no. I wouldn't send any of my Jinn to her." Marsum snorted. "It was of no benefit to me."

Of course that was the reason why.

Maks slid out of the crevice and stretched, his vertebrae popping and cracking as he drew in a deep breath. Above him the jagged rocks presented plenty of handholds and toe footings to climb. The more concerning part of the climb would be being seen and picked off before he made it to a window.

And then that window needed to be in a place that he could hunker down and work from.

"Fuck," he whispered as his hands bled and ached. The longer he waited, the worse the pain would get. If he missed, though, or slipped off the edge of the window he'd be dead. For real this time

He wiped his hands one at a time on his shirt, in an attempt to take the worst of the blood off. That was all he could do, though.

One deep breath and he leapt out for the window

ledge. His fingers slid sideways, and he bit back on a scream as his body went.

"Pull hard," Marsum said as if he were training Maks once more.

Flexing his body, the momentum of the slip still there, he curled his feet toward his head and the window ledge. The world tipped upside down and then as suddenly as he'd been sliding to his death, he was on his knees and staring out at the crashing waves.

He scooted backward and bumped into a closed window. "I can't believe that worked."

"Me either."

Maks glared at his father. "And you didn't think to talk me out of it?"

Marsum shrugged. "It was that or the water, and we both know you wouldn't have made it far. You might be able to swim, but you live in a desert. It is not a strong skill of yours. Never mind the beasts that live below the waves."

Not wrong, the ass was not wrong.

Turning, Maks fumbled with the window, managing to get it open. He slid into the dark room, closed the window behind him and took a deep breath.

Ointments and herbs, the faint tang of a wood flame.

He was in the apothecary of the white-haired old woman who'd made the drugs for him so her mistress could bang him.

A low string of curses whipped out of him as he

searched the room for a hiding place, a weapon, anything that could help.

Across the worktable were a few small knives—nothing that he would consider better than his fists—crushed herbs, powders, and a piece of paper with scrawled words he could not decipher, the edges burnt.

Footsteps turned his head and he shifted, diving for the cover under the low shelves on the darker side of the room.

"Idiot girl!" The door flung open and a waft of fresh air came in with her. Maks watched, eyes narrowed so as to not pick up the gleam of any candles. "She thinks I can just drag in another Jinn like this?" She snapped her bony fingers for good measure. "Kindness, and food. If she'd done a little work, that last one would have been putty in her hands. But no, she wants to break them, to force them to love her!"

Her words were not exactly quiet. He wondered just how dangerous this old woman was, seeing as she didn't seem particularly afraid of the Storm Queen. Her feet drew close to the shelving unit he was under and he pulled back further while Marsum chuckled in the background.

The old woman paused. "Who is there?"

Sweet goddess in a basket, would he never get a break? He was not about to answer her, but if she felt his presence then . . .

"Arin," Marsum said. "It's been a long while."

"Jinn! What. . . how are you here?"

She could see Marsum? Or just hear him?

"That was my son that leapt from the castle," he said. "I seem to be stuck here now."

Arin snorted. "You be stuck wherever you want to be stuck. That's how it is with a pure-blooded Jinn. Just like Dani. She chooses this place and this life."

The old woman walked away from the shelving unit and Maks dared to peek out a little as her back was turned. She went to the worktable. "She is blind. Just like you."

"I was captive to my ancestors," Marsum said. "A little different—"

"She is captive too, just with a responsibility that she wishes to see through. But she cannot find a black unicorn. That would bring her a step closer to fulfilling the prophecy. Of ending Asag and his reign so she could be queen of the east, as she was born to be. This mess of wanting a child is a fool's hope. That will come later. If she survives. Right now, she needs a strong Jinn with her to face Asag. If I can convince her that is."

Maks couldn't believe she spoke so freely, but then she thought Marsum dead, and no other to listen.

Or did she? She came back to the shelving unit and crouched down. Her hand shot toward him and dragged him out from his hiding place. He shifted and stood in front of her, his hands going around her neck. Could he kill her?

She smiled up at him. "You want to get out of here alive, you're going to need to work with me, boy."

"I won't fuck her."

Her smile widened. "Do as I say, and I'll help you survive Dani and her whims. And maybe, just maybe, you'll get to keep your life after too."

15

ZAM

With my eyes closed I let myself feel the movement of the dragon under me, and the way that Vahab's hands clung to my body. Lilith raged from her place on my back and yet that rage was distant.

In the quiet of my mind, I knew only one thing.

Vahab was a dead Jinn the second I had the chance.

I had no doubt that Lila would be chasing after us, but she was also carrying Reyhan and that extra weight would slow my friend down. Which meant for the moment, I was on my own.

I sunk deeper and deeper into that state of quiet, feeling it cover me like a wave through the river. I found myself holding my breath for long periods of time as if I were indeed swimming, as if I were once more in the river below the Nasnas monster.

And I waited for my moment. Patience was not a

virtue of mine, but the injuries from the Ijiraq were not small. The poison from the beast was burning through me still, more like an infection. Nothing like the bite of the rabisu.

Patience. That's all I needed.

"There, Fen," Vahab hollered. "Between those two valleys looks fine by me. A lovely place for a union of souls, don't you think?"

If I could have gagged, I would have. Union of souls my lily-white ass. I was going to show him a union between my fist and his face.

"Are you sure?" Fen's muscles tightened below me, the uncertainty in his voice clearly audible. "I'm not sure that she wants this."

"Why?" That Vahab even asked the question was interesting.

"I think she has a mate, Vahab. And I can sense her small dragon still following us despite the child she is carrying. Which means that she will not be alone . . ."

"Are you saying that you can't kill that five-pound dragon?" Vahab laughed. "Wait . . . do you like her? Please tell me you are not so foolish as to get your heart involved. Again. You do recall how that went for you the last time you let your emotions lead."

Fen flinched and I rolled my wrist so that I could put my palm against his hide. Because the energy he was throwing off, I knew it well and it struck a chord with me.

Shame.

Shame that he'd made a wrong choice in a mate. Shame that he'd not been able to see that his choice would never have worked no matter how hard he'd tried. I pressed a little harder with my hand because while I couldn't quite find my voice, I did understand what Fen was going through.

Vahab laughed. "You have the worst instincts in a dragon I have ever met, do you know that? That pipsqueak of a dragon back there is nothing more than a runt. She is no dragon even! A lizard at best! A snake with legs!"

Fen was quiet as we descended out of the clouds.

I kept my hand against his scales and felt him calm a little.

We dropped to the ground, and I kept my eyes closed. The infection was raging—the fever running through me was climbing rapidly—but that didn't mean I couldn't fight.

We will kill him. I will run him through. Cut him into pieces, bleed him dry!

Lilith was only a little pissed, by the sound of it. Though at that moment I wasn't all that bothered by her murderous rhetoric.

I breathed through the growing rage, pushing it aside as best I could. Rage had a place, I knew that. But I also knew that I would have limited energy to deal with Vahab. And he was the *first* Jinn. No matter what he'd said so far about his abilities, I didn't quite believe him. Which meant that I had to be smart about this.

Smart and fast.

A pang around my heart and there was a moment in my mind where I saw Maks, curled up as a caracal in a small rock crevice, the water of a wrathful ocean blasting around him. His eyes were closed as if he were asleep. Ears pinned back to his head.

Next to him stood a man I knew all too well. Marsum. He lifted a hand to me and waved. Then winked as if . . . as if all were well.

Shit, what was happening if Marsum had shown back up in Maks's life?

The moment slid away as Vahab pulled me off Fen's back, slung me over his shoulder and started walking, my head lolling and bouncing against his upper thigh. Where the hell did he think he was taking me exactly?

"I know you won't understand," he said as he adjusted his hold so that his hand was gripping my ass cheek, massaging it. "But this is how it must be. You are the only Jinn woman I've seen so much of a whisper of since I've been free, and I've been searching the dream-scape at night. And it is the union of the strongest male Jinn and the strongest female Jinn that is needed to stop Asag." He dumped me off his shoulder and I hit the ground hard, knocking what was left of my air out of me.

Blinking, I stared up at him. "What?"

He shrugged out of his shirt and tossed it on the ground. His ribs were clearly visible and not in a trim, I've got all these muscles kind of way. More in a I've been starving for years kind of way. Scrawny, he was damn scrawny.

"I'm not overly happy about it either," he said, and that was evidenced by the lack of arousal in his loose pants. He put his hands on his hips and shook his head at me, as I were the problem. "You want to stop Asag? We need to get flouncing."

I managed to hold a hand up as the screaming banshee that was Lila came in like a goddess-damned tornado. She dropped Reyhan onto my belly and shot up between me and Vahab.

"One more step toward her and you'll be picking up your face in pieces!" she screamed.

Vahab rolled his eyes. "Fen. Remove her."

I turned to see Fen hesitate. More than hesitate, he didn't move. "I . . ."

"FEN!" Vahab twisted around and glared at his dragon, hands on his bony hips. "Remove her now! We are wasting time and Asag will figure out that I am free soon!"

Fen was shaking and I could see the war in his face. Lila didn't even look at him.

How much hurt had happened between the two of them in their combined pasts? Too much.

"He cares for her," I said. "You can't force him any more than you can force me into your bed. At least not without a fight that will leave you bleeding out on the ground."

Vahab threw his hands in the air. "Save me from dragons who can't control their hearts!"

"Never," I whispered.

Lila shot a look at Fen. "I won't give up my sister for you."

He shook his head, took a breath and moved to stand behind us. "I . . . I am with you, Lila. I am with you." The hesitancy, and the bravery it took for him to utter those words, I could only imagine.

But they were the words that she and I spoke to one another. I am here. I am with you. They almost meant more than I love you, at least to me. Love could be fickle. It could lie and tell you that someone like Steve was amazing. It could make you believe in a person who wasn't worth believing in.

To stand with the person you cared for? To hold their hand in their darkest hours? That was strength. That is the power of a bond that goes beyond love and beyond fear. It is true magic.

And it was there, growing between them—Lila and Fen. I let my eyes drift shut to see the bonds that tied me to my lion pride, something I'd not done in a long time. *That* magic hadn't been taken from me, at least.

Bright lines connected Lila and Reyhan to me. But a faint line also connected Fen to Lila, shimmery and hesitant, but very much there. He was growing on her.

I turned my head to follow the gold line that stretched from my heart to the south. Toward Maks.

Why had I not thought to use this sooner? Because

I'd been relying on bigger magic, on bigger power to get me through. The smaller things, and the things that mattered had slipped away.

Maks was alive and well. I could feel him through that cord connecting us, so maybe that vision of him and Marsum had been a glimpse of the truth. I wobbled to my feet, clutching Reyhan. She turned herself toward Vahab and hissed. "You are outnumbered," I said.

Vahab put his hands to his head. "And just how would you like to stop Asag then? The prophecy calls for a rider on a black horse, a union of the strongest Jinn, and a dragon! All the pieces are here!"

I took some pity on him. "You aren't even attracted to me, are you?"

"Of course I'm not! You . . . you're a mess! You have no power that I can see and that is incredibly unattractive to me. And you're all muscle! Your curves are nonexistent! I like some shape on my woman!"

I could have laughed at him.

If he wanted a strong female Jinn, then I would give him one. I glanced at Lila. She was fighting a smirk and I could almost see her thinking. Give him what he wanted then, see if the fool liked his other option.

I was rapidly losing energy, so I gave him the carrot that I suspected if I dangled it in front of him, he'd take. "And if I said there was a stronger female Jinn? One who has power that you've even tasted but maybe didn't recognize?"

He twisted around and frowned at me. "What kind of power?"

"The Storm Queen," I said. "She is Jinn. She made that ice storm that sent Fen to us, and had us cowering in a cave for hours. She controls the rhuk."

Vahab held his discarded shirt in one hand, but I could see by the tension in his body that he was considering what I was saying.

"How can you be sure?"

I let out a breath, feeling the danger of the moment slipping by. He would not try and flounce me. Hell, he didn't even want to, despite what Lilith had predicted. Then again, that was likely her game. To set me on edge, to make me think that he would kill me if I didn't fuck him.

"Because her power feels like mine, or at least part of mine," I said. "And I'm just . . . well, I'm a mutt. I am part Jinn, but I'm part shifter too, a little bit of fairy, and apparently the heart of a dragon." I lifted my hand to Lila and pulled her to me.

She flipped off Vahab as she wrapped herself around my shoulder. "Remember when I said you should kick Fen out of the cave, and you felt sorry for him?"

I wasn't going to argue with her that if I hadn't done that, Fen wouldn't be standing with us, against Vahab right then.

"You were right to bring him in," she said. Fen

brightened at her words, his scales actually shimmering a deeper green.

It was so cute it was gag worthy.

Vahab kicked at a few rocks. "What are you suggesting then?"

For the first time I felt like I was seeing the real Vahab. A man desperate enough to stop Asag that he would do the things he didn't want to. Despite the fact that I was that thing he didn't want to do, I could see that he was serious.

"A partnership in truth from here on out. No more lies. No more games. No more tactics. We both have the same goal—to bring Asag down. The Storm Queen has my mate. He is also half Jinn." I thought about what she wanted from him, and for a moment I could almost feel the story come together. The heat from my fever spiked and I knew I had to focus on the first step. "Help me take down Asag. Not by fucking me, but by getting me to my mate."

"Flouncing each other, that is the only way." The frustration in his voice was obvious.

"Unless you bang the Storm Queen," Lila said. "I do believe that's what Zam is getting at. If you want a powerhouse of a Jinn woman, the Storm Queen is your girl."

I nodded and went to my knees, then back onto my butt. My throat was tight and hot, as if I'd been sucking in fumes from a fire. Lila kept talking.

"You get the Storm Queen, and we get Maks back."

Lila stayed close to my face. "Then we move on Asag together. A team."

Vahab was quiet. "That . . . makes sense. No more games. I will be true to this pact. We will go to the Storm Queen, and I will have her in my bed. Then we will deal with the demon."

"You do whatever you want to her," Lila muttered, "long as we get Maks."

I smiled and closed my eyes. This was good. We were going to work together finally. Maybe I'd forgive Vahab at some point for the bullshit he'd put me through and the ass grabbing.

I will never forgive him! Lilith's scream was there, and I cringed, unable to fight it off.

Lila's claws slid over my face, poking at me. "But first we have to take care of Zam. She's running a high fever. That venom is really doing a bang-up job on her."

After that, things got . . . blurry is the best word. Hot and cold at turns, I know I thrashed and flopped on the ground like a fish out of water. Hands covered me with blankets or doused me with cold cloths depending on my temperature.

Lila was a constant presence. Reyhan was a constant presence, and for the first time in a long, long time, I let the bonds to my family pride open. That opening allowed me to feel their emotions and their worry, but also allowed me to pull a little strength from them to boost my healing.

Not once since Asag had taken my power had I

thought to reach back to my roots, and yet they were still there. I could feel my brother Bryce, Shem, Kiara . . . I could feel Maks and his frustration, I could even feel the Emperor—my grandfather—distantly. They were there and as I fought against the infection their strength flowed to me. A trickle from each of them that maybe none would notice.

No, that wasn't true. Bryce noticed. In the fog of my mind I saw him as he lifted his head and turned his golden eyes my way. My brother knew I was in trouble. I don't know how much he saw, if he saw only the infection or more. If he knew that I was facing a demon.

"Zamira." He growled my name. "We will come. We are family and we stand together."

"No!" I lifted my hand to stop him. Not because I didn't want his help. But because I could not bear to see his peace shattered once more. "No, stay! I can't . . . I don't want you in danger again!"

But he was gone, determination set into his face.

Damn him.

I did not want to bring my brother or our family into this any more than I already had. And yet . . . I could already feel the shifting of the desert sands, swirling as change settled in on my life once more.

My family was coming to me.

Whether I liked it or not.

16

I woke up, fever free, in the early hours of the morning when the night still reigned but the sun was peeking up at the edge of the horizon. Reyhan was curled up in her cub form in the crook of my arm, sound asleep. Lila was in the crook of my neck and Fen ... Fen was wrapped around all of us.

"I see you are finally awake," Vahab said. "Which is good because I think we need to get moving." He handed me a flask and something that I assumed was food. I took a swig of the drink.

Tepid water, but there was some sort of herb in it giving it a good tang.

"Drink it all," Vahab said. "You need it. You sweated out most of your water."

He was being ... normal. Was this the real Vahab? I hoped so, because I needed someone to work with me, not someone I had to ass kick every five minutes.

"What's this?" I motioned with my hand holding the jerky.

"Camel, I think." He shrugged. "We took it off some scavengers while you were out. Or more accurately, your Lila took it."

I took a bite and chewed it a minute before shaking my head. "Not camel." There was a gamey flavor that hung in the meat that was barely covered up by the serious amount of salt that had been used in preparing it. But I didn't care what it was made from at that point. My belly was happy to have something in it, even if it was a mystery meat.

I sat up slowly, felt a wash of dizziness but it fled as I got my bearings. "How long was I out?" I drank down the last of the water and handed it back to Vahab.

"Not as long as I thought you'd be. You drew off your people."

I was on my feet in a flash. "How did you know that?"

"Lila said she could feel you taking a little from all of your family," Fen said as he lifted his head. "I think that's why she and the child are still asleep."

I scooped up Lila and Reyhan. They were out cold. "I took too much."

"You are alive." Vahab straightened his ragged shirt as if it were a much nicer outfit. "If the cost is they sleep the day away, it is a rather small price to pay."

Fen bobbed his head in agreement. "I felt a little of it too, but I don't know how that can be?"

I wasn't about to spill Lila's secret. "Maybe because I understand what it is when you love the wrong person."

Fen closed his eyes. "You think Lila is wrong for me?"

Shit, did he really think he loved her already? I mean, in part I understood, she was fucking amazing. "No, I mean whoever hurt you. Lila wouldn't do that. She doesn't have it in her to break hearts."

Fen's eyes filled with what I could only guess was relief. And maybe a bit of hope.

"Okay, enough therapy for today." Vahab clapped his hands together. "Let's go."

Let's go turned out to be us climbing on Fen's back. "I thought you couldn't carry this much weight," I said as I settled in behind Vahab, Lila in my hood, and Reyhan tucked tight in my arms.

"He lied," Vahab said. "Because I didn't want to move too fast."

Fen leapt into the sky, different than Lila would have in her larger size. Instead of powering up, he kind of galloped forward, undulating and picking up speed before he was rising. His body undulated through the air, his long white mane fluttering around us.

"The prophecy," I yelled into the wind. "What do you know of it?"

"It's not a prophecy," Vahab yelled back. "Or at least not the way you might think of it." He twisted around to look at me. "Demons have a set of rules and if those rules aren't followed, they are automatically sent back through the Veil to their realm."

I frowned, thinking about Asag and Mamitu, about Pazuzu. "You mean like his three challenges that have to be faced in order to then face him?"

He nodded. "Yes, exactly. The natural world demands balance, predators and prey, or things go to shit. He is a predator. But that means he has to have at least a weakness that his prey can manipulate if they are smart enough."

The wind warmed as we wove our way through the mountain passes. We weren't very high, at least I could see the valley floors and the . . . "Oh shit, those are pillars."

Asag's rock monsters were swarming in the same general direction as us, just further below. If one of them looked up, we were screwed in the most royal of senses.

"I can help with that," Fen said, and a mist swirled out around his mouth, sweeping out and closing us up in what was essentially a moving cloud bank.

Lila stirred from my hood. "They aren't seeking us by sight but tracking the kid by some other way."

"It can't hurt," Fen said.

Unless they started shooting at us.

On cue, a flaming arrow blitzed through the cloud bank, and just missed Fen's head. "Shit!"

"Out of the clouds," I said. "We can't avoid the shots if we can't see them coming."

Fen dropped, diving straight for the ground, which meant we all got a little air. I clamped my legs around his middle at the last second and clung to his mane. Vahab squealed and floated above Fen's back until Lila shot forward and landed on his shoulder, shoving him back down.

"Hang on," Fen yelled as he began to spiral. The momentum was intense, and I closed my eyes so I didn't lose my lunch.

Nope, that wasn't any better. Nausea flipped my stomach upside down, as Fen did the same thing. I could feel the burning arrows going past us, the heat of the flames kissing against my exposed skin, but nothing landed. I opened my eyes to the world twisting in and around itself.

Fen grunted once, but that was it.

He pulled up hard above the floor of the valley between the mountains and skimmed along. Looking over my shoulder, there were no pillars.

"Where did they go?"

"I threw my mist around them. They are blind for the moment," Fen said.

"It won't last," Lila said. "They aren't tracking by sight, which I believe we've already covered."

He shot a look back at her. "It's the best I can do."

"Seems like you are lacking then," Lila muttered and I . . . I really wasn't sure why she was being a jerk.

"Maybe you want to stop them?" Fen snapped.

"Maybe I will!" she snapped back.

"Lila, you don't have enough—" I was going to say acid.

"Enough what?" she growled. "Size? Strength?"

Oh boy. "We've tried killing them before and even your acid doesn't make much of a dent, which means we need to be smart about this. What can stop a fucking rock monster?"

Silence all around as we flew hard. Ahead of us the edge of the desert was showing through, glimpses of the sand here and there.

Balder and Dancer would be there, which meant we'd have the speed we needed.

My brain hurt as I tried to figure out just what the fuck we were going to do. The rock monsters would keep coming, all the way to the sea if we didn't stop them. And I had no desire to be stuck between rhuk and a rock monster, with a storm on top of us.

"We have to find a way to stop them," I said.

"And just how do you propose to do that?" Vahab said.

I reached up and touched Lila. "I think I need to walk the dreamscape."

"Right now?" Vahab bellowed.

"Who do you know that has any knowledge about Asag who can actually speak without getting caught up in some sort of binding spell?" I yelled back. "I . . . I will speak with someone I know that has been around a long time."

Lila clawed at my neck. "You think that's a good idea?"

I shrugged. "It's all I've got for ideas other than trying to outrun them, which we know won't work long term."

Her hold on my neck eased and she grunted. "This is stupid. I hate that demon and his stupid rock monsters." I reached up and patted her on the head.

"We'll figure this out, we always do, right?"

She shot me a look. Yeah, I wasn't feeling all that hot shit right then either, but I wasn't about to let Vahab know that. Much as we were technically working together, let's be honest, the trust just wasn't there yet.

"I can see the horses," Fen called over his shoulder. "We are almost to them."

Just ahead I could see the body of the rhuk, Cassandra, her wings spread wide as if sheltering her chicks. Or in this case, the two horses.

As Fen landed and slid to a stop I was off and running toward Balder, Reyhan still sound asleep in my arms. I'd give the kid that, she was able to sleep through anything.

"Balder, get ready to run!"

He reared up, spun and went to one knee, lowering his back for me. I leapt, landed in the saddle and we were off.

Cassandra let out a screech. "What about me?"

"Can you keep up?"

"Of course!" Her launch into the air sent a curl of

dust and sand around us, but I closed my eyes and leaned into Balder, kissing at him.

Lila clung to my neck. "You think you can fall asleep while we run for our lives?"

"The herbs that Pazuzu gave Reyhan to keep her quiet." I reached under my shirt and pulled the pack of nepeta out—catnip. As Balder galloped flat out, I grabbed my water bottle and sloppily mixed the nepeta into it, and gave it a shake.

I looked at Lila who sat on the front of my saddle watching me. "Bottoms up."

I chugged the water. The tang of the herb was unpleasant, but within seconds my limbs loosened.

Oh, I had not thought this through.

"Lila . . ." I slurred her name as I slumped forward.

"I got you, go find us help!" Her claws dug into me and then I felt a hand on my right side, holding me in the saddle.

Vahab was beside us, the black mare bringing him alongside me and Balder. That was all the coherent awake thoughts I had before I slid into the dreamscape.

The world was the same and yet not. I watched from the back of Balder to see the army of Asag in the distance and losing ground. But that wouldn't last.

I leapt off his back and kind of floated for a minute in space before dropping to the ground. Something inside of me shifted.

Nope. Not quite like that. The head of a tiny jungle cub stuck out of the top of my shirt. I pulled

Reyhan out and she shifted to two legs. "Where are we?"

Jaysus on a crippled donkey. I hadn't even thought that Reyhan might be able to dream walk with me. I decided my best shot was to explain quickly as we moved. I took her by the hand and started running.

"We're going to find help, and this is a dreamworld where things can still hurt or even kill us, but we can also do some pretty amazing things."

The scenery around us blurred as we ran.

She laughed and giggled. "This is great! If I yell fuck here, can anyone hear me?"

I stumbled. "I can hear you!" I looked at her. "And we don't say fuck."

She grinned up at me, just the bright little girl she was, without the dark shadows of being hunted by rabisu, or Asag, or having lost her entire family.

"Where are we going?"

I thought about the person I was hoping could help. "A wise woman named Flora. She . . . she might know something about Asag and his monsters."

"So that we can stop them?"

I squeezed her hand and nodded. "Yes."

The landscape shifted suddenly and I was no longer in a desert, a jungle, or a mountain top.

I was in a place I'd never seen, but had heard about. A city. But not like a desert city; one of the cities that had been on the Indiana Jones documentary with thousands of people, and buildings taller than any mountain.

At least there were no people here.

"Flora?" I hollered her name. Of course, she had to be sleeping too. Damn it, there were too many holes in this plan of mine. That's what I got for making a decision on the fly without considering how it could backfire.

"I don't like this place," Reyhan whispered. "Where are we?"

I searched the signage around us. "Seattle."

I paused and headed toward the smells of something nothing short of magical and found myself stepping through a door into a bakery. "Oh my goddess," I whispered. The stacks of delicate pastries, the smell of fresh bread, the pull of food made by the hand of a . . . well, of a goddess, made my stomach rumble.

"Can we eat it?" Reyhan whispered.

"No," I said. "We have to find Flora."

"Flora isn't here." The dulcet alto voice turned me around. A woman stood there, looking at me, looking at her. She had long black hair, green eyes, and weirdly looked a bit like me. Only she was much taller and had the body of a . . . well, of a goddess. Maybe this was the one who'd done the baking?

"Who are you?"

"I'm Flora's granddaughter, Alena." As she spoke her image wavered. "She only just got back home from her trip. Did she meet you there?"

I nodded. "I need to ask her a question."

"Maybe you can ask me?" Alena offered. Again, her image wavered, and she stretched, a self-satisfied smile on her lips. "Remo, don't wake me up."

I frowned. "I doubt you'd know. No offense."

She shrugged. "None taken, I'll tell my grandmother you were looking for her." And then she was gone.

I turned and pulled Reyhan with me. "I want to stay!" she whispered.

"I know, but it's not real. We can't eat it."

She sighed and I felt the disappointment myself—not only for the food but for not finding Flora. Because my other option . . . was my grandfather.

"Okay," I whispered more to myself than to Reyhan, "let's go find the old bastard."

17

Reyhan and I blitzed away from the place called Seattle. Before, the dreamscape had been set only in our world, over the desert. Something had changed if we could walk through the entire world. Or maybe that was what happened when my grandfather's hold on the place slid.

"Who is the old bastard?" Reyhan asked.

"My grandfather." I jumped over the ocean of water, barely registering the impossible move. Weird how this world worked, because it could kill us and a fall from this height normally would. I didn't want to dwell too much on the mechanics of the place I didn't fully trust or understand. I would just take it as it came.

"And he can help us?"

"I hope so."

Focusing on the Emperor, I found myself being

drawn back to a place I don't think I'd ever truly believed I would return to.

The Stockyards.

The home of Ish, the home of the Bright Lion Pride. The place I'd lived for most of my life. I found my feet slowing as we drew close to the buildings. There was not a lot of movement here, other than a few animals scurrying about.

"Shax, I need to speak with you." I used his given name because I wasn't sure that I wanted to call him Grandfather. Or the Emperor. Neither really fit him.

"What if he's not here?" Reyhan whispered.

"Then we keep looking," I said with a great deal of confidence, enough that she smiled even while inside I could feel my guts twisting. There were not a lot of options when it came to long-lived beings that I could trust. Or that I hadn't already killed.

I let myself in through the front door, and was immediately assaulted by memories. Of Steve and Kiara. Of my brother injured. Of Ish . . . I shook it off. "Shax?"

A scuffle came from what had been the main meeting room. "I am here."

Still holding Reyhan's hand, I led the way through the double doors and into the room. Braziers were lit around the edges, giving off only a little heat, but a great deal of light. Carpets littered the floor, softening our footsteps.

My grandfather, stripped of all his power, sat in the center of the carpets cross-legged and with his hands resting on his knees. "Zamira."

"This is the old bastard?" Reyhan whispered, but of course she was audible, loud and clear.

His bushy white eyebrows climbed to his hairline. "I suppose I am the old bastard. Did you have a child? No, it can't be, she is too old."

"I am protecting her from Asag," I said, watching him for a response.

And boy, did I get one.

His whole body tensed and he paled so far that I thought he was going to fall over. "The demon?"

"You know him then?" I lowered myself across from him and for just a moment I could feel the movement of Balder under me, galloping at high speed while I made this journey. Strange to be in two places at once.

"I know him. He was . . . part of the issues I dealt with in my early years as the Emperor. And he was part of the reason we chose to wall off the eastern and western desert from one another."

"We."

"Myself, and a few others who chose to remain there, to try and stop him." He shrugged. "They would be gone now, Asag would have killed them."

I nodded, even though I suspected that Mamitu, Pazuzu and Vahab might actually be the ones he was speaking of. "Asag has sent his pillars after us."

Shax frowned and touched a hand to his chin. "I do not know of such things."

I thought about it. "That is what the locals call them."

"It's a stupid name," he pointed out. "Describe them to me."

Reyhan cleared her throat. "They are rock monsters, and they can't be killed and they are his army. And I hate the fuckers."

He choked on a laugh. "Ah, so then that is something I know a little of. They are a type of golem. Not sentient, not thinking on their own. Perfect for a demon like Asag." He rubbed his face again. "How many of them are there now?"

"Hundreds."

A grimace crossed his face. "That does not bode well. And they have been around for thousands of years, so I would guess that they are no longer soft clay, but hardened rock and stone?"

"Yes!" I leaned forward. "Almost impossible to hurt, or stop."

I can hurt them.

Lilith's voice caught me off guard and I flinched. My grandfather noticed. "What is it?"

"A new weapon," I said. "Sister to the flail."

He sighed. "You do not need to challenge yourself every time, you know. I know that weapon, she is far more dangerous even than your flail."

It was my turn to grimace. "I wasn't aiming for a challenge. I was aiming for a weapon that wouldn't be a pain in my ass. And I know that she is worse, I've experienced it."

Lilith let out a laugh that had me shaking my head.

"Back to Asag and his golems," Shax said. "What do you need to know? How to kill them?"

I nodded. "Yes. They are hunting," I almost said Reyhan's name, but instead shot a quick look to the top of her head. "Us."

My grandfather gave a low sigh. "Asag is unredeemable. He always favored the young ones. His golems have a weakness, but it is not an easy one to make happen, I think."

"Anything. We need something," I said.

The old bastard clapped his hands together three times, and a brazier rose up in front of him, the flames blue and green. "What destroys clay?"

I blinked at the flames, undulating like the waves of an ocean. "Water."

"No blade will kill them, no acid will eat through their outer shells. You must wash them away." He rolled his hand through the flames. "How you will convince them of that is where things could get interesting. They are, of course, fearful of water and avoid it at all costs."

"And they can fly," I said. "So even if they got close to water, they can fly over it."

"Interesting, that is a new trick then." He bobbed

his head and yawned. "I hope that helps you, grand-daughter of mine."

I almost nodded. Almost. "What do I owe you for this information?"

He smiled. "You know me too well. I will call on you, should a need arise."

Damn it, I should have negotiated at the beginning, but I was in too big of a hurry. Also I was trying to figure out just how we were going to make this happen —getting Asag's entire army into water.

"Maybe we can make a trap for them?" Reyhan asked as we stood and the world of the dreamscape wobbled around us. The nepeta was wearing off.

I closed my eyes and forced myself to wake up, dragging Reyhan with me once more into the waking world. Groggy, the motion of Balder racing along had me bobbing and struggling to sit upright. Okay, maybe the herb wasn't wearing off quite as quick as I thought.

Lila pinched my cheek. "You've only been gone a couple minutes, what did you learn?"

"Water," I whispered. "We need a fuck ton of water."

"Do you think we could piss off the Storm Queen? Have her send a deluge our way?" Lila asked.

It was a good question but I already knew the answer. "She wouldn't save us, not after trying so hard to kill us. And the last thing we need is to be stuck between a Storm Queen and Asag's army."

"Good point," Lila said. "So what's the plan then?"

I looked south. "Straight to the ocean."

WE GALLOPED the horses as hard as we dared, for as long as we dared. Until I was sure that there was nothing left in all of us. I told them what little I'd learned. Vahab had grunted, but didn't disagree. Had he known?

"There. That's as good a place as any." I pointed to the faint trickle of a stream pouring out of a section of rocks and down into a small pool. Water was good for all the reasons the desert demanded. But now that I knew that Asag's golem army could be killed, or at least melted away with it, I found myself desiring it even more.

Water was life in the desert, now in more ways than one.

I stripped the horses of their tack as they dropped their muzzles into the pool of water and drained it down three times over. I rubbed them with the one brush I had, knocking the sweat and dirt off, then fed them a handful of oat balls before they wandered off to graze on the few grasses nearby. The pool and small waterfall had created a mini oasis that we were going to take full advantage of.

"So how do we get an entire army wet?" Lila asked. "I mean all in all, this is great, but how do we actually implement it?"

"That's the question of the day," I said as I scooped up a flask of water for Reyhan first and let her chug it down before I took my own drink. Lila pulled the dried meat and flatbread out of the saddlebags and handed it out, and the group of us sat down with an audible sigh.

Vahab shook his head. "The ocean is not that far away. Perhaps we just keep riding hard."

"The horses don't have weeks of hard riding in them at this point," I said. "They have a few days and I don't know that we are that close."

I closed my eyes and reached for the connection to Maks that I had. That golden thread lit up so that when I opened my eyes, I could see it still. Distance was harder to figure out, but we were closer. More than that, he was not afraid. A little confused, but not afraid and not hurt. That was good.

A few minutes later Cassandra landed, her wingtips brushing across us all. "You are hard to keep up with! They run like unicorns!"

My lips twitched. "Something like that."

She settled herself down, still towering above us all. Her talons were huge and I found myself staring at them. She could carry a horse in each talon.

Excitement shot through me. "Cassandra, how many rhuk are there left that don't belong to the Storm Queen?"

She blinked her gigantic eyes a few times. "Maybe a dozen. They are the old females that are no longer laying eggs. Useless."

I stared up at her. "Think they'd want to put a dent in Asag's day?"

Cassandra clacked her beak and leaned down close to me. "What are you thinking?"

While Maks was not entirely sure he trusted Arin, or her motives, she had been true to her word. She'd kept him hidden from Dani and her raging.

"You wonder why I am keeping you." She didn't look up from her workbench where she was hunched over a basin. Stirring and adding, stirring some more. It smelled like shit to Maks but Arin kept tasting it and muttering under her breath. "And I will tell you again, that my reasons will come clear soon. I have to convince my Dani of something first."

"Good luck with that," he muttered. His spot in the corner was such that he could not see the door should it open, with the large armoire between him and it. In terms of safety, it was probably the best he was going to get.

Arin laughed, a cackle that made his hair stand up along the back of his neck. "I will tell her to seek the oasis of dreams, boy. And if you are truly Marsum's son, then you can help take her there. I have seen the future in the oasis, and I know it to be true. My Dani will die if she keeps on this path, thinking she can take down the demon."

He had to force himself not to perk up. To act like he had no idea what that might mean. "What demon?"

"Asag. He rules the City of Sorrows, and in turn rules all the world except," she held up a finger, "the Kingdom of Storms. We have held this stronghold for generations against his army. They fear us."

Interesting. But it didn't help him out at all. "What about this oasis of dreams?"

"A place where your future is laid out if you remain on the path that you stand on now." She purred and dropped a charred bit of bone into the basin. Smoke curled up, smelling like cinnamon. "But you cannot go alone. You must go with another Jinn." Her eyes shot his way. "Preferably one that has walked in the dream-scape before."

"And you assume I have?"

"I can see it on you. Those that have walked the dreamscape look beyond the world as it is, as if they know already there is more if they only stare hard enough." She tipped the basin up and poured it into a decanter, stuffed a few flower petals in and shook it violently. The mud-brown liquid swirled and slid until it became a light indigo, filled with tiny specks of red and blue.

"And that?"

"Oh, this is an aphrodisiac for the guard." She motioned her head toward the door. "Something to keep him busy while we go find Dani."

He swallowed hard. "Now?"

"Yes, now."

"I don't trust that she won't kill me on sight," he said.

Arin sighed and the door clicked. He watched as she turned to face her visitor, her face smoothing. "Granddaughter."

Fuck.

"Old woman, I cannot find a Jinn worth his salt that will fuck me!" Dani threw herself to the floor . . . sobbing.

Maks pulled back further into his small corner as if he could hide there permanently. He would not say he was a coward. But with no magic to his name, and no way to even escape, the anxiety riding him was like nothing he'd felt in a very long time. Not since Marsum had used to corner him as a child and beat him.

"Now, that's not fair," Marsum said. "It wasn't me. Not really." His father leaned next to him.

Maks kept his eyes locked on the dark-haired woman on the floor. She was kneeling, and bent forward in a child's pose. As if in supplication to her grandmother.

"And if I told you that you should never be concerned about fucking a Jinn again?" Arin said. "That a Jinn would only bring ruin and destruction on you, our home, and our people?"

Dani lay still. "The prophecy—"

"May not refer to you at all!" Arin snapped. "You are not the only female Jinn alive, Dani."

"I am queen here . . ." She began to raise herself up and Arin slapped the back of her head.

"You may be queen, but you will listen to me now. Go to the oasis of dreams, go and see for yourself what future awaits you on this path."

Dani rubbed the back of her head. "And how do you want me to do that without an escort?"

"I have gotten one for you," Arin said. "I saved him myself."

Maks didn't dare snort. But he did stop cringing. The last thing he wanted to look like in front of a volatile woman like the Storm Queen was a cringing weak man.

Dani finally lifted her head and Arin pointed at him. Dani's eyes bugged out and her jaw dropped. "I saw him land on the rocks below!"

"And I said to you that I myself have saved him." Arin smiled.

Maks didn't want to point out that a strange pair of

demons had been the ones to save him. Call him crazy, but that might not help his case any.

What he didn't expect was for Dani to lose her mind. Again.

Screaming, she launched herself at him. He caught her hands and swung her around to slam her into the wall.

"Enough!" Arin shrieked, as if they were naughty children.

Outside the skies darkened, and in seconds the rain had opened up on the world.

"You are the reason I am barren!" she screamed in his face.

"You're barren because you're a raging psycho!" he yelled.

She tried to kick him in the balls, and he twisted sideways to take the blow on his hip and thigh. He yanked her close, spun her around and shoved her face against the wall while he continued to hold her hands tight with one hand.

Before she truly used her magic on him, he had to knock her out.

"Do not hurt her!" Arin yelled and something slammed into the back of his head.

A frying pan? That was his only thought as he slid sideways.

No, the basin she'd been working in. Some of the liquid ran down the side of his face and his last thought before he hit the floor was two-fold.

One. Do not let that liquid into your mouth.

Two. This had to be the craziest family he'd ever met in his life. And that was saying something. He'd met Lila's father, after all.

WHEN HE CAME to there was something cold on the back of his head and the sound of hushed feminine voices rolled around him.

"I am telling you that he can take you to the oasis and it will open for you then," Arin said.

"I would rather kill him than have him be my escort. He called me a psycho!" Dani snapped and there was the sound of glass breaking.

"That won't help my opinion," he mumbled before he could catch himself.

Arin laughed.

Dani growled something under her breath and beside him Marsum sighed. "You always did like to do things the hard way."

Maks slowly sat up. They were still in Arin's work room, and it hadn't changed much if you didn't count the fact that almost every glass bottle had been broken. The sound of the rain on the roof was not easing off either, and the wind had picked up in the time he'd been out cold.

Arin snapped her fingers at him. "Granddaughter, he can walk you through the oasis. If he doesn't, you can still kill him."

Dani paced the room, her gauzy skirts floating out around her, flashing the fact that she was completely bare underneath.

He looked away.

"What, am I so vile to your eyes that you can't even enjoy a free show?" She came to a stop in front of him. He could have kept his mouth shut. Probably should have, but he'd been with Zam and Lila too long to let an opportunity to sass an asshole pass him by.

"I would not want the free show unless I were blind."

Arin snorted. "Oh, I do not want to like you, boy."

Dani whipped a hand out to slap him and he caught her by the wrist and stood up, dragging her upward until she dangled above the ground. "Do not raise your hand to me again." And he gave her a shake, as is she were a naughty cub.

Her eyes dilated. "I wish you would fuck me."

Grimacing, he dropped her and stepped back. "If I help you go to this oasis, I want passage to the mainland."

Dani didn't look away from him, her mouth parted and eyes locked on his body.

Arin gave a nod. "You have my word that if you help her walk the oasis of dreams, that you will be given passage to the mainland."

He held a finger up. "Alive."

The old woman cackled. "Alive then, fine. So picky you are."

Dani closed her eyes. "Fine. I will take him with me. But no matter what the oasis shows, I will have my way, old woman. I will be the one to kill Asag."

Maks looked at her and forced himself to hold a hand to her. "Then let us be done with it."

19

The night passed far quicker than I wished. Cassandra left as soon as I explained to her what I was hoping to do. If she could gather the other rhuk, the ones that the Storm Queen had discarded, we might have a chance.

"If I were big, I could do it," Lila grumbled from where she'd curled up next to me. "But I bet that's why Asag takes everyone's magic when they step into the desert."

"I know, friend," I said. "But with a dozen rhuk, we might be able to make this happen." I paused. "And you're right. Asag takes everyone's power right away because it reduces the chance that he's going to have his ass handed to him."

The rhuk were our only real hope and they weren't a for-sure. They were a might. A maybe. A possibly.

None of those words were great when describing our future, but it was all we had.

The golem army was seeking out Reyhan, and maybe I'd pissed off Asag enough that he was looking for me too. Either way, they were coming for us, and we had a way—maybe—to stop them.

Gods above and below, I hated that word.

I leaned back and closed my eyes.

The waiting for a battle was the hardest part. More so when the sword you carried decided to speak up and keep you up all fucking night.

Perhaps a truce between us?

"No," I mumbled.

Lila grunted and curled in tighter to my side.

Please.

Damn it. It was the politeness that got me. "What do you want to say, Lilith?"

Yes, I said her name out loud so everyone would be on their guard. If I wasn't going to rest, no one else was either.

Revenge is all I have. There is nothing left of me of the woman I once was. But I can make you stronger. And without you, I cannot be anything. You have not drawn me as your weapon since . . .

"Since you made me go crazy? Yeah, that's the thing, losing control is death in our world. I can't trust you," I said and settled more onto my side so the sword sheath didn't dig into my back.

She was quiet a moment and I could almost feel her thinking, as if she were squirming inside the blade. Not a pleasant feeling to be sure.

I can be nothing but what I am.

"Which is the problem." I drew a breath and sunk a little deeper into the sand at the edge of the pool.

But when you are ready to kill Asag, you will need all the strength you can get. Will you promise me to draw me as your weapon then?

"What is she saying?" Vahab asked. "Promising she won't drive you bonkers and make you kill all of us while we sleep? Do not believe her."

I repeated to him what she'd said about Asag, which seemed to surprise him if his silence was any indication. "Can I trust her word on that?"

"No," Vahab said. "But she always hated Asag. We had that in common. It was what drew us to one another. Comrades more than lovers. So perhaps on this she might be a tad more trustworthy when it comes to promising to kill Asag." He held his finger and thumb about an inch apart.

I could see that. Lilith was . . . intense was perhaps the best word. Her sincerity was there in how she felt. Then again, her power in taking over me had felt very real and sincere in its way too.

"I cannot promise you that I will ever pull you from your sheath again," I said, considering how to spin what I wanted to say. "But I will consider it if you prove yourself helpful."

Again, she was quiet. She waited until the others went to sleep, I could hear it in their breathing. I wondered how aware she was of the others. If she could hear their heartbeats or some such.

I can help you find Asag. That will be the final test after all three challenges are met. It is why I was created. A part of the puzzle that is sending him back to the realm of demons was also to have a single way to find him. That way is me.

I didn't answer her, but waited quietly for her to continue speaking. She sighed, the ripple of it down my spine a rather odd sensation. As if she were giving up something.

I am bound to him, the way you are bound to your dragon. He was part of my family. I . . . am a demon.

My eyes flew open. A demon. Strapped to my back. It took all I had not to fling her from me and run in the opposite direction. Instead I stood, careful not to disturb Reyhan or Lila, and made my way off to the north, walking briskly.

What will you do with that information?

I walked until I was sure Lila and the others would not hear me and still I kept my voice low. "You're a goddess-damned demon?"

I am.

I wrapped my fingers around the back of my neck and stared up into the starry sky, struggling to breathe through the horror. No wonder she'd taken me over so easily. That was what demons did. They possessed people and forced them to their knees. "You say you will help me find him, but I am guessing that there is a bargain here. If what Vahab and the others have been saying is right, there is always a way to deal with a demon. So, what is your deal?"

I told you, I wish to be used to kill Asag. Her voice had not changed in inflection or tone, and yet my gut told me that she wasn't being entirely honest. Shocking, I know.

"There is something you aren't telling me about that," I said.

What happens to me when I kill Asag is between me and our parents.

Our.

"You're his sister?" I breathed out the question and could feel her sigh again.

I am. And he is my destiny in more ways than one.

This was a whole lot of nope in my world. "And you would kill him."

He has done this to me. Has made me a part of his game, believing that I would never find it in me to kill him. You either end his life with me, or you will not end him at all. There is no other weapon that can be used on him. Though not very many know this.

I paced a circle around a thorn bush. That would mean I would have to practice pulling her free and working with her. I had to willingly work with a demon, to kill a nastier demon. I grimaced.

Before I could think better of it, I pulled her free of the sheath on my back. "You can change shapes?"

Yes.

"Can you make yourself into a flail?"

Lilith shivered in my hand. The length of the handle stretched out and the metal of the blade shimmered and reformed into a spiked ball that dangled from a chain. The handle was polished wood, and the steel of the spiked ball was a dusky gray without an ounce of shine to it. I rolled my wrist and the chain clanged as I spun it round.

You are more comfortable with this shape?

I slid through the movements I'd trained when using the flail. Step, spin, switch hands, spin again. Lilith and her machinations were quiet as I moved through the exercises. Breathing through them and waiting for her to try and take me over.

"Okay, let's try," I said.

You wish me to . . . try and possess you?

I gritted my teeth. "Yes."

I'd barely said the word and the world blacked out. When I came to I was standing over a sleeping Vahab, my arm pulled back and ready to let fly with the flail.

I opened my hand and dropped Lilith. Letting out a breath, I realized that miraculously, Vahab had not woken up.

"That was stupid," Lila said.

"Yeah." I turned to her, wondering if I was as pale as I felt. "I need you to be my second while I train with her, Lila."

She snorted. "And do what? I don't want to spit acid

on you and with her in your hands, I don't particularly want to get bashed either."

Gingerly I reached down and picked up Lilith and walked back out into the desert away from the camp. Lila flew after me, looping through the air. She was thinner than I'd ever seen her and I was suddenly, acutely aware of how much stress we'd all been under.

How little we'd eaten, drunk, or slept in weeks.

Back out by the thorn bush I stopped. "Lila, you can stop me. Use the connection between us."

Lila landed on top of the center of the thorn bush and tucked her wings in. "Okay, but I still think it's a bad idea."

You must . . . embrace me, instead of fighting me, Lilith said.

That sounded like a terrible idea. I closed my eyes and nodded.

And woke up walking back toward the camp.

Lila could snap me out of the fog that Lilith put me under, but that was the only good thing. Two hours we trained before I called it.

"I can't stop her," I said as we stood there by the thorn bush. "She's too strong."

"You are stronger," Lila said. "You withstood Jinn trying to take you over!"

"But Jinn . . . they aren't a demon."

Lila leapt across the bush and I caught her in my arms and hugged her tight. For the first time in a long time, I was afraid. Afraid that we weren't going to be able to finish this journey. Afraid that Asag and his golem army would win. And worse, I was afraid that I was once more that weak shifter who was not strong enough to save her friends.

Lila slapped my face. "I know that look, knock that shit off right now."

My jaw dropped and she grabbed my face with her tiny claws. "You are still the same Zamira I met at the edge of the Dragon's Ground. Fierce and smart, and tough. Maybe we don't know the path we are walking, but that's never stopped us before. So. Stop it. Stop doubting yourself."

I gave a tired laugh. "Lila, what would I do without you?"

She arched her eyebrows at me. "Probably die."

We will keep practicing.

Lilith's voice was not tired, but I could feel the frustration in her. I swung the flail up and over my shoulder, and like the first one, it locked into the sheath with some sort of magic. Good enough.

"We should get some sleep." I turned and started back toward our camp.

Lila yawned. "A few hours would be good. We'll try again. You'll get this. I know you will."

My sister-friend's belief in me was a balm to my soul and yet I knew the truth. When it came to Lilith, I wasn't strong enough to stop her from taking me over fully.

Which meant that there was no way I could use her against Asag.

20

Two hours of sleep was not enough, but it was what we got. Reyhan woke me up, tugging on my ears. "I'm hungry and there is a dust storm coming."

I rolled to my feet before I was fully awake, my body registering that her words made no sense. There was no wind. "Go to the saddlebags, eat something," I said as I stared north. North where the golem army was even now working their way toward us.

Sand and dust rose up from their hundreds and hundreds of feet.

"Let's move." I ran to the horses and saddled them both up before Vahab even opened his eyes.

"Five more minutes."

"That's fine, you do that." I didn't want to point out that he probably wasn't on the army's hit list anyway.

I grabbed Reyhan and swung her up on Balder's back before joining her. With a grumble Vahab mounted up on the black mare, Fen small once more, wrapped tight around his neck.

"Lila?"

"I'm going to swing back and see how many there are." She was gone before I could tell her no.

"Damn it," I muttered.

"I'll go with her!" Fen released his hold on Vahab and shot away, shifting in size as he left us. He shot straight across to meet Lila and then veered away. I could only imagine the thrashing she was giving him.

"Let's go." I bumped Balder with my heels, and he picked up a quick trot. I didn't want to race ahead. Not with Lila and Fen back there.

Vahab rode up beside me. "Do you think the rhuk will help?"

I shrugged. "I've no idea. But I've got nothing else."

The Jinn nodded, his face solemn. "If we get to the water, maybe the Storm Queen will help."

I snorted. "She tried to kill me once already."

"You think that was all for you?" Vahab asked. "Don't you think highly of yourself."

"You got a better explanation?" I asked. "She just happened to have a bad PMS day and tried to wipe out that particular part of the desert?" I lifted my eyebrow at him. "Fuck that particular lizard right . . . there."

Vahab laughed. "I still don't think it was for you. My delicate flower wouldn't do that."

Good grief, he was already falling for her, and he'd not even met her. "Be careful, you might create something in your head that is not even close to reality. What if she's all muscles and lean like me?"

He grimaced, his lips curling up like he'd smelled a pile of rank camel shit. Yeah, that was what I thought. His imagination was surely running away with him. But then again, maybe so was mine.

There was no reason for me to think that indeed the storm had been all for me, but I suspected it—the storm had felt directed at us. What better way to make Maks open to her advances than to take me out of the picture?

What if Maks thought I was dead?

That thought was a hammer between the eyes, and I gasped. If he thought I was dead, then he might have slept with her. For his freedom and his life, it would be a small ask if his mate was gone. Even if he hated the woman who'd done it.

My stomach rolled and I had to shake my head to clear the traitorous thoughts. If he had . . . and he believed it gained him his freedom, I could understand.

Whatever it took to survive, that was the code of the desert.

Biting back those vile thoughts, I looked over my shoulder, reaching for the connection between Lila and myself. She was okay, irritated but okay.

From what I could tell the dust cloud hadn't gained

on us, and we hadn't gained on them. That was good enough for now.

And I would think no more of Maks fucking the Storm Queen and just focus on the shit we were sinking in.

We continued on at that pace. Reyhan had picked up on a constant stream of consciousness that flowed out of her mouth. Vahab stared at her. "Is this normal? Is she broken?"

Reyhan didn't seem to even notice as she started rhyming words over and over in a singsong.

"It's been a long time since I've been around young ones," I said. "But generally they love annoying adults."

Reyhan giggled and snuck a look at me, and I gave her a squeeze. She was a good kid, smart and brave. Which made the idea of Asag stealing her away even more horrifying. He'd destroy her not only in her body, but her heart and mind too.

A whoosh of wings turned my head as Lila landed on Balder's rump. "There are a lot of them."

Fen landed a moment later on the black mare's saddle. "I'd guess close to five hundred. I feel like they are picking up numbers, they seem to be coming in from all directions."

"And they are holding back on their speed while they do it," Lila said, her jewel-toned eyes full of worry. She shook her head. "You think Cassandra will pull through for us?"

I didn't know how close we were to the ocean, or

how far away Cassandra was, but water was our only hope, even if we had to ride straight into it. "We ride hard now," I said. "And hope we can make it to the water in time."

I turned away from the army at our back and gave Balder his head, kissing at him. He and the black mare leapt forward in tandem and we were off and running.

Torin had run for me like this, faster and faster, but he was a fully mature adult stallion. One that still had his horn.

"Go as long as you can, my friend," I yelled into the wind. Balder bobbed his head once and then stuck his nose straight out as he reached for a longer stride.

Lila crawled around to sit in Reyhan's arms. The little girl was quiet now.

Even she could feel the danger that was coming for us. I didn't dare look back. Not yet.

That moment would come soon enough.

WE RODE HARD, only stopping where we had to for the horses to drink. Three times I got off and ran beside Balder, and made Vahab do the same. He grumbled but otherwise did as he was told.

Thank the gods, because I wasn't sure I could deal with another problem right then.

"Um . . ." Lila said as we were galloping up to the top of a slick sand dune. "I think we have a problem."

"Tell me it's not a new one." I leaned into Balder's

neck, trying to keep my body more in line with his as we took the hill.

"Well . . . kind of?" She hovered just above me and was staring not behind us, but in front of us.

Balder reached the top of the hill, breathing hard, sweat slicking his body. I reined him in, and we sat at the top of the dune staring at what lay in front of us.

Blue water, cresting with white curls as they dashed in across the sand. How in the world could this be bad?

Lila grabbed my head and turned me ever so slightly to the left. Out in the water was an island capped with a massive castle that rose up into the lower clouds.

Lightning crackled above the peaks of the roof and the wind snapped away from the castle and straight toward us. More than that was the number of rhuk roosting along the edges of the castle.

Well fuck.

"I thought you said that it was further east than we were headed?" I barked at Vahab.

"Well, I guess I was wrong then!" He smiled. Smiled. Mother fucker . . . he'd done it on purpose to get us closer to his girlfriend. "You said you needed us to get to water fast, that's what I did."

I spun in my saddle and punched him in the side of the head. "The problem is she doesn't know that you're coming to woo her! She'll see us as intruders, you dumbass!"

He howled. "But she'll see the golems as intruders too!"

She also had been hunting for the horses—aka hornless unicorns. I slid off Balder's back. "My friend, you have to go."

I stripped him quickly of his gear, pushed Vahab off the back of the mare and did the same to her. "Go, find somewhere safe and I will find you." I kissed him on the nose and saw Reyhan do the same to the mare.

He snorted once, and I thought he'd argue about leaving me. But this time he did not. In a flurry of sand and hooves he was gone, racing down the side of the dune and heading east. I almost called him back until I saw him angle away from the water. That would have to be good enough.

We were done running from the golems. One way or another we had to stop them.

I scooped up the saddlebags and left the rest of the gear behind. Lila flitted around my head. "Battle it is."

I nodded. I did not see this ending well. And what would I do with the girl if we were overrun?

She skipped ahead of me, her long hair tangling in the wind. She didn't truly understand what was happening. Or what Asag would do to her.

"Lila, if it gets tight, you understand we can't let her be taken."

Lila closed her eyes and Fen gave a low growl. "You can't be serious."

I rounded on the other dragon. "And what would you do? Let him have her?"

Vahab hunched his shoulders, but I said nothing to him. There was nothing to say. We were literally between a roost of rhuk and an army made of stone and clay.

He did not like this. Stripped to the waist, the old woman had drawn swirls and designs all around his torso and back, over his face and down his arms. "You will be first into the water. And if the magic recognizes you as one who has walked the dreamscape before, then you will easily take my Dani to see her future."

Maks said nothing. There was nothing left to say. Either he helped these crazy women do what they needed to do, and he was set free, or . . . or he was back on the chopping block.

They stood in what felt like the lowest floor of the castle. Arin had blindfolded him and led him to this place, down twisting staircases and through a number of doors. She'd even backtracked twice, and he thought it was to throw him off until she began muttering under her breath.

She'd gotten lost. Whatever this place was, it was hidden well, even from those familiar with it.

"Take her through, and then bring her back." Arin patted him on the shoulder on one of the few spots that he was not covered in swirls of red and black paint.

Where they stood now was a circular room that had been carved out of rock. Water dribbled down the walls, dripping and cooling the already damp room. Three torches flickered against the walls, sizzling and dancing as water caught the edge of the flames.

"Anything else?" he asked, more out of habit than a real desire for direction.

"Do not touch it," she said.

He didn't have a chance to ask what 'it' was. The scrape of the rock doorway turned them both around. Dani stepped through, only her face covered in the same swirls that he was. With a shrug of her shoulders her gown slid off and she stood naked in front of him.

He turned away. Apparently the 'it' was Dani.

The Storm Queen stepped up beside him. "You, into the water first."

"What water?" The floor was solid rock and the only water he could see was that which dripped down the side walls.

Arin pointed at the center of the floor and the rock slid sideways to reveal a dark pool of water. There was no light, no way to tell the depth of it. Being from the desert, water was not a favorite thing of his. He could swim but . . .

The old woman snapped her fingers. "Into the pool."

A fear that he would jump into the pool, and they would slam the lid shut was a rather sudden and unpleasant thought. Jaw tight, he stepped toward the edge and then stepped out over the water.

He held his breath as he went down into the pool. The water was cool, not cold. He bobbed back to the surface as Dani dropped a rope over his neck and tied it to her wrist. Right before she dove in next to him.

The rope tightened and he took a gulp of air before he was diving down with her, chasing her.

This was a terrible idea. He swam hard after her, keeping the leash she had on him loose. It took him a minute to realize that there was light under the water, and that he could see they were headed toward the glowing source of said light. At the bottom of the pool was a sandy beach and . . . trees? How was that possible?

Dani reached the beach first and swam toward it. The world seemed to turn upside down and they went from swimming through the water to stumbling across the beach. Or at least he did.

"What . . . ?"

"I have never been here," Dani said. "But my grandmother has spoken of her one journey here, many years ago. I knew that it would be strange and beautiful."

That was an understatement. All around he could see water, as though they were inside a glass bowl.

He moved to take the leash off his neck and she yanked it tight, dropping him to his knees. "You will come with me and you will not take that off. It is all that ties us together. That and the symbols we both wear. Without them, this construct would come to pieces and we would both be destroyed."

"Listen to her," Marsum said, strolling alongside him. "She's not wrong about that part."

Maks got to his feet and banked his anger. "You could have just told me."

Dani sniffed and Marsum shrugged.

The sand was warm under his bare feet as they walked away from the edge of this . . . construct, as she'd called it. The sand headed downhill and soon gave way to grasses, trees, lush fruit bushes and even the call of birds. A soft breeze brought the smell of rain on the horizon, and the sweet scent of ripe fruit.

"Here." Dani tugged on his leash, leading him down the hill further. At the base of the hill was a small pool of water. Only this one had nothing natural about it. Instead, it was a fountain that had been made out of a solid gemstone. Carved like a stemless glass, water pooled in the center of it, bubbling ever so slightly.

Dani approached it and he could smell the fear on her.

"What happens now?" he asked.

"I drink the water. Then I will sleep and while I sleep I will dream in this place of my future." She knelt next to the sparkling chalice and cupped her hands into the water. Hesitating, she stared for a solid minute at it before she brought it to her lips and swallowed it down.

Maks was not sure what he was expecting, but when she slumped sideways he was still caught off guard. She hit the sand and he stared at her as her breathing deepened.

"Well, isn't this fun?" he muttered as he lowered himself to the ground. He wasn't sure if he believed her about staying tied together, but just in case he would stay close.

"Life rarely is." Marsum sat beside him.

He looked at his father. "You said your goodbyes before, why are you really back?"

Marsum laughed but didn't meet his eyes. "You think I should have stayed away?"

"I think it's weird," Maks said. "You've been helpful and not helpful. You know a hell of a lot more about this side of the desert than you have in the past. Were you lying before?"

He shook his head. "Ah, boy, you don't understand. I want you to succeed. I want you to take down Asag. That is important for the world, for the desert. For every supernatural—including the Jinn."

Maks frowned harder. "Why, Marsum? How did you know so much about Nico and Soleil? How did you know that they needed bodies to possess if they were to come forward again? That they were looking at me and Zam to be those bodies?"

His father's jaw ticked. "Just because you think you know everything—"

"I don't." Maks cut his father off. "What I want to know is who you really are? My father is gone, I felt him leave."

His father—or at least the entity pretending to be his father—went very still. "You figured it out. I'm impressed. I did not think you were close enough to him to realize the differences."

"I've been suspicious, but the reality is you haven't done anything harmful. So let us be true between one another, who are you?" He motioned with a hand at the sleeping body of the Storm Queen. "Do you have a connection to her?"

Marsum shook his head. "No. I . . . was a Jinn. I was killed trying to protect my family from Asag many years ago. You slept on my grave and your own pain woke me as nothing else would have. I saw in you a chance."

"And?"

"And I would help you stop Asag. I know demons well, boy. Better than most." He sighed. "My name is Roshawn, and I was a hunter of demons. We were a sect of the Jinn, created and trained to take them down. And in turn, we were hunted by Asag and his army."

"And you chose to help me why again?" Even though Roshawn's words made sense, he needed to understand truly why it was him and not someone else.

Roshawn smiled at him. "Because you share my

blood, boy, you share the blood of a demon hunter. Your pain, the loss of your mate called to my own pain and woke me from a long slumber."

He stared at the figure next to him. The face that had been Marsum's shifted, sliding into a longer, narrower chin and nose, dark brown hair past his shoulders, dark brown eyes, and deeply tanned skin. Roshawn was leaner than both Maks and Marsum. "Are you a shifter too?"

"No, I am not." Roshawn ran a hand over his head. "We need to get you away from this one, though."

"You said you didn't know her," Maks reminded him.

"No, I don't. But I knew her grandmother. They are a long line of female Jinn, powerful in their own right." He glanced at the chalice that Dani had drunk from. "Mostly because of that."

Maks crouched next to the chalice but didn't touch it. "What is it?"

"The source of all magic. And the thing that Asag wants more than anything else in the world."

Maks turned and stared at the item in question. He couldn't take his eyes from the chalice once he'd truly looked at it. Cut out of what looked to be a diamond, it glittered and sparkled with the small amount of water in it. "And if I drank from it?" What he was hoping was that perhaps his own magic would be opened back to him. So that he would not be so helpless when dealing with Dani.

"Do not. The fact that she dared to even put her face in it," he waved a hand at the still-sleeping Storm Queen, "is surprising. But then again, you are both covered in protective symbols meant to guide the magic."

"I felt nothing," Maks pointed out.

"Doesn't matter, the magic was directed at her. She didn't really need you for this. Have you ever even walked the dreamscape?"

Maks frowned. "Not like Zam."

"Exactly. This is a game to Arin. Whatever reason she wants you here for is not what she's been telling you, and it's not what she's been telling her grand-daughter. When you get out of this place," Roshawn waved his hand at the oasis, "take the first boat off the island. The demons wait for you there, not here."

"Wait, demons?" Maks spun on his heels, and Roshawn was gone, and Maks had a feeling it could be for good. Dani, on the other hand, was slowly waking, a groan sliding out of her.

He didn't touch her but stood and stepped away. He wanted nothing to do with the Jinn woman, any more than he had to in order to get away and get back to Zam. His heart thumped hard at the thought that he might be too late, but he knew it wasn't true. He'd felt her at the other end of their connection. She'd been hurt and drawing on him without realizing it.

"I'd know," he whispered to himself.

"Know what?" Dani rolled and sat up.

"If my mate were dead." He watched her as she rubbed the side of her face.

Dani stood and wobbled, putting her hands out, but he didn't help her. "I learned much. We must go. My plans have changed."

That had to be good. He let himself feel a small amount of relief. She tugged on his leash and began to walk back up the slope that led out of the oasis valley and to the edge of the water. She put her toes into the surf, and he followed suit.

Once more the world turned upside down and then they were swimming hard for the surface, toward the flickering lights of the torches.

Dani popped her head out first and he swam up next to her, dragging himself out before she even got the rest of her body clear. He did not trust her not to lock him in there.

"What did you learn?" Arin asked her granddaughter.

"Much. You were right, the path I am on must change." She wiped her face, the fatigue written clearly across it.

He slipped the leash off his neck and tossed it to the floor. "I have done my part. Arin, you swore to me I would leave on the next boat."

The old woman nodded. "I did. But I do not rule here."

Dani turned to him. "I might need to walk the oasis dreamscape again. And it showed me that a child of yours would be a great boon to this world. So, I will take my time with you."

He stared at her, anger surfing its way to the top of his body, coiling his muscles tight and his fists tighter. "I will not."

"You will." Dani's voice was calmer than he'd ever heard it. "I saw it in the dreamscape. A daughter, just as I'd hoped."

And just like that, his own hopes were dashed, gone on the winds of a storm he could not fight. Which meant all he could do was hope that Zam was coming to get him.

The edge of the Sea of Storms lapped at my boots. We were here, and Asag's golem army was coming. Vahab stood next to me, his hands on his hips. "Now what?"

"We hold our ground and hope to hell the rhuk show up," I said.

Reyhan played and jumped in the waves. I wasn't sure she was all that oblivious to what was happening, but maybe she knew this might be her last time to play. My throat tightened. That could not be. I couldn't let it be. I swallowed hard. "One of the dragons has to take her out into the ocean. Not too far, maybe twenty feet."

Lila tightened her hold on my shoulder. "I will take her. And I . . . I will do what I must if it comes to that."

I nodded, unable to speak. "I will shift. As a jungle cat I have the strength and bite to throw them into the waves."

Interesting that Lilith didn't argue with me. Even what she could do as a magical weapon wouldn't touch the golems.

Vahab snorted. "And me? You don't expect me to help, do you?" Even as he spoke he started walking down the beach, away from us. "I only said we would work together to get here. Nothing more."

I stared at him. What a shithead. There was nothing I could do to make him stay. To make him help us. I turned my back on him. "Come not between a dragon and his wrath."

Lila grunted. "That's a good one."

Fen's body shimmered as he shifted into his larger version of himself. "I will stay, I am with you. I can grab them and throw them into the water."

I lifted a hand and he put his nose against it, his warm breath curling around me and sending his long white moustache fluttering in the wind. "Thank you, Fen."

Lila reached out and mimicked me. "Yes, thank you, Fen. Maybe I was wrong about you. Maybe you aren't so bad after all."

The green tinge of his skin deepened, and he turned away. "I am not the monster you think I am, Lila. One day I hope you will see that."

Her skin deepened too with that, and she looked away, a distinct sparkle of tears in her eyes. Perhaps this was more of a heart twist than I'd realized.

Vahab wandered off a few steps and then stopped. "Perhaps I will watch, to see how the fight goes."

"Whatever floats your boat," I muttered.

The thing about a fight, a battle, is that the waiting is the hardest part. My belly twisted in on itself and I had to force myself to eat a little, and drink down some water. Because once the fighting started, there would be no break, no time out to catch our breath. Either we would win the day, or Asag would have us. I could not see any other outcome, which terrified me.

Fen and me against an army of five hundred. This was not going to be a good day, no matter how it went.

"You know, we could have run straight toward the Storm Queen," Vahab said. "I am sure she would side with you."

I rolled my eyes. "Your fantasy woman does not exist. For all you know, she works with Asag and would hand us over to him."

"Cassandra said she didn't," Fen pointed out.

I wanted to tell them they were wrong, but maybe they weren't. I forced myself to look at the island out deep in the ocean, the waves crashing around it. I could feel Maks stronger than ever before and he was there. Waiting for me.

Held captive by a woman actively trying to fuck him. My anger surged and I pushed it down. "Lila, if it comes to the worst, fly Reyhan to the Storm Queen. Beg protection."

Lila's mouth dropped. "What?"

I nodded, feeling the certainty behind what I was saying. "That is the answer. If it comes to it, if we are overrun, take her to the Storm Queen."

A rumble under our feet turned us all around to face the northern sand dunes. At the top of the final dune appeared the first of the golem army. "Pillars, what a stupid name," I muttered.

Lila grimaced. "Whoever named them had not so much brain as ear wax."

I paused, letting my mind work over the quote. "Troilus and Cressida?"

"Damn it, I'm never going to stump you, I could only stump Toad!" Lila spun around, weaving her way through the air currents. Her anxiety was showing in her barrel rolls again.

A smile crossed my lips even as more of the golems gathered. "You've been saving that one, haven't you?"

"Damn skippy I have." She sighed and dropped onto Reyhan's shoulder. The little girl reached up and patted her side.

"Zam," Reyhan said, and I turned to her. "The monsters are after me, aren't they?"

There was no denying it and I did not like lying, especially to a child. I nodded. "Yes, but we're going to make sure you are safe, the best way we can. Okay?"

She frowned. "But if you can't—"

"Then I will fly you to safety." Lila butted her head against the little girl's. "You will be okay, Reyhan."

Her eyes went to Vahab where he stood a little apart

from us. "Are you going to protect me too? Are you going to help keep me safe?"

His face said it all. Shame was a heavy thing to swallow and he sure tried if the way his throat bobbed was any indication.

Vahab went to one knee and held out a hand to her. "You . . . trust me? No one else does."

He wasn't wrong about that last bit.

"You're the first Jinn," she said as she put her small hand in his. "You could kick everyone's ass if you wanted to."

His laughter was unexpected and he tugged the girl into his arms for a quick hug. "Because you asked so sweetly, yes. I will stand with these three and you of course, princess." He flicked his fingers at me and Fen and Lila.

"Am I a princess?" Reyhan gasped, and Vahab nodded.

"I deem you first princess of the desert Jinn!" He touched her on the head and a tiny burst of sparkles spread out over her face.

She gasped and spun. I turned back to the sand dune where the golem army still gathered; they stood ten across. Ten across meant there were at least fifty rows deep of golems.

Fuck.

The one in the front raised his arm and spoke.

"Give the girl to me, Vahab. And I will not pursue your death."

Vahab put his hands to his chest. "You think I've been doing this? You're a fool still, demon. I am no Roshawn the Deadly, hunter of demons. I am the one you caged, and I am just glad to be free. Also this one," he pointed at me, "is a pain in the ass. I don't much like her."

The golem opened its mouth and laughed, a horrible grinding noise of rock on rock that stopped as suddenly as it had started. "Then give them both to me. Then we will be quits."

"It's not up to him." I snapped the words out, feeling my own anger climb my spine and pour out of my mouth. "Your army is dead today, Asag. And then I'm coming for you. I've released Vahab. I know where the source of magic lies. The tasks are nothing to me."

I wondered if his face was tightening. If Asag—wherever he sat watching this through his creation's eyes—was having a fit, throwing chairs around because of my defiance. I hoped so. And that hope made me smile.

"Why do you smile?"

"Because you think you've got us pinned down. You think you've won before the battle even begins. But you don't know me. You don't know Lila. You don't know what we've survived."

The golem pointed a hand at me. "Every survivor dies at some point. Every fighter collapses one day. This is that day."

"Want to make a bet on that?" Lila zipped around in

front of me and the urge to grab her tail and tell her to be quiet was so strong I lifted my hand before I clamped down on it.

Your dragon is clever. Make a bet with him, he loves to gamble. All demons do.

Lilith's words were spoken with more than a little excitement.

"Yes, a bet," I said, and Lila looked back at me. I gave her a nod. If she had an idea, I trusted her enough to run with it.

The golem's eyes went dark and I thought that perhaps we'd pushed Asag too far. But a moment later, a creature I knew all too well emerged from between the golems.

"Mamitu?" Her face was littered with bruises. "Fuck."

The graceful woman walked down the slope, her red skirts spilling out around her. At the bottom of the dune, she held out her hands and before I could ask, her eyes shimmered and changed to orange.

"Do you see," her voice was deep and thick with Asag's tones, "that I keep what is mine. Forever. Mamitu made a bet against me and she lost. Do you wish to make the same mistake?"

If he is trying to talk you out of a bet, he is afraid you might have a chance to win. Which means the rhuk might be close.

Might. Maybe. There were those words again.

"If we beat your army today, you will free Mamitu, and no longer pursue the child," I said.

She swivelled her head side to side. "And you? Do you not wish me to stop pursuing you?"

I let a slow, angry smile cross my face, so that he could see my teeth. "I am coming for you, either way, Asag. I do not care if you chase me all the way to your doorstep, demon."

Mamitu's face darkened. "You . . . do not fear me."

I did because I was no fool. But I wasn't about to tell this dumbass that. Instead, I dug deep and pulled on every ounce of badass that I'd earned.

"See me trembling? I'm shaking like a leaf." Maybe I could goad him into this fight.

He flicked Mamitu's hand at me and I was swept up into the air, my limbs pulled in all four directions until my joints popped free. A scream bubbled up in my throat, but I would not give him the satisfaction. I would not scream for him. Instead I closed my eyes and let the tears run down my face, silent.

"If you beat me, you may have Mamitu's freedom. And I will rescind my desire for the girl. But you . . . you I will gladly take. Let us begin this bet in truth."

As quickly as I was tossed into the air, I was released.

"Oh camel piss! He popped all your joints out!" Lila dropped next to me on the sand. There was only one way for me to deal with this. I needed to shift.

I walked through that door in my mind between

shapes and a moment later I was shaking sand out of my black fur and standing comfortably on all four legs.

"Keep her safe," I growled to Lila and butted my head against hers.

"Don't die on me," Lila said. "We've done this too many times to lose now."

I really hoped she was right.

I turned as the first ten golems came marching down the dune. Vahab cracked his knuckles.

But it was Fen who took them first. He shot into the sky, undulating and flinging his body around to gain height, then swooped down from the east and grabbed three of the golems fast and hard, banked and dove straight into the water.

He was gone in a massive splash and didn't come up.

"Fen!" Lila shot toward the place he'd gone down.

I didn't have time to watch to see if he was okay.

The first golem reached me, and I dodged its sword and grabbed its leg, dragging it toward the water, my claws digging in far deeper to the stone and clay than I thought they would. Then again, I was carrying Lilith when I shifted.

I am lending you my strength.

The golem tumbled under my efforts, and a foot and knee touched the edge of the waves.

And those parts completely disintegrated. The golem stumbled up, one-footed and off balance as it turned away from the water.

"Hell no." I leapt up and grabbed onto its back and then threw myself backward. Already off balance, the golem flailed and fell with me into the shallows.

Reyhan squealed. "That's so good!"

"Lila, get her out of here!" I snarled as I leapt toward the next golem. This one was flying at me, parallel to the ground, fist straight at my head.

I jumped straight up and landed on its back and shoved it down into the water. A quick glance at Vahab showed me that he was flinging the creatures out into the water with a quick snap of his hands and whatever magic he had left to him.

Golem after golem came at us. Fen did get out of the water and grabbed more. But with each golem we tossed, we ended up taking blows too.

Gashes down my side, my face, a tooth knocked out, more and more came. More and more injuries flowed.

I lost count and could no longer see through one eye. Blood dripped down my skull when Mamitu lifted her hand.

"Pause."

Pause. What the hell kind of shit was this now?

I looked over at Mamitu with my one eye, and her glowing orange eyes that told me Asag was in charge. No surprise there. I didn't actually expect him to leave the party early.

"Pause? No one pauses in the middle of a fight!" Vahab yelled. I could hear the fatigue in his voice. The golem army had been coming at us nonstop. The position of the sun told me we'd been at this for at least four hours. My legs and muscles agreed with that assessment and begged me to just lie down in the wet sand.

"Can you not see that I have been kind?" Mamitu purred as she spread her hands wide. "I have let the golems come to you, only a few at a time. Allowed you to think that you could survive." I swallowed hard, knowing that what Asag said through Mamitu was true. "I have held them back when I could have unleashed them fully. Now that you are somewhat fatigued, perhaps you would like to revisit our bet? Perhaps you'd like to just give the girl to me and I will let you go?"

"No." I growled the one word but didn't dare shift back to two legs. Simply because I was not sure I would have the energy to shift back. How long before Cassandra found us? Goddess above and below, she was our only hope now.

Mamitu laughed. "You will be fun to break, Zamira Reckless Wilson. I will have you both by the end of this."

The fact that he knew my full name was only a little unnerving. I took the moment as I could, breathing deeply and snagging a bit of jerky from my saddlebags, swallowing it whole. I glanced over at Vahab and Fen. The dragon sat on the edge of the shoreline, his body as bruised and battered as mine, blood running freely down his sides. He and I were not using magic to launch the golems, and the bastards were hard with their blows.

Lila hovered just above Reyhan who stood knee deep in the water, her eyes wide as she hugged her own body, shivering. If I sent her now, the golems would chase her and take them down before they reached the Storm Queen—assuming of course that the Storm Queen would give the child safety.

"You think that there are only five hundred of my creations, that is amusing," Mamitu said. She clasped her hands behind her back. "Five hundred is not even close to what is out there. Waiting for you. Obeying me."

When was it time to throw the towel in? Not yet. It could not be yet. I looked at Fen and Vahab and they both gave me a slow nod. We were good. For a little longer at least.

"Are you tired?" I asked him. "Because it sounds like to me you are afraid of losing and are trying to hedge your bets."

Excellent. He hates it when women think him weak.

Mamitu's eyes changed from orange to her own color. "Zamira, be careful!" And then she was gone again, orange eyes blazing. "She thinks herself clever, that one. Clever is a very undesirable trait in my women. You should remember that when I am riding you. I like my women quiet."

I grimaced. "You're disgusting."

"And yet you parlay with me? You talk with me, why?"

I bared my teeth at him as the heavenly sound of wings reached my ears and my hopes flared. "Because I'm buying time for my reinforcements to show up."

He fled Mamitu and one of his golem's eyes turned orange a split second before he turned to look back the way they'd come. Mamitu slumped to her hands and knees. "Zamira, the girl is not his goal any longer. You have intrigued him too much. Defied him, and he wants only to break you. Get the child out of here now while he is not looking, and she will be safe with the Storm Queen. I swear it." Her eyes fluttered and she hit the sand, face down.

"Reyhan, shift! Lila, you heard her, fly to the Storm Queen, go!" I tipped my head and Lila was already scooping up Reyhan, in her cub form, and flying hard across the water. There was no time for goodbyes. No time to wonder if it was the right choice. It was the chance we'd been waiting for.

The strangled screech of a rhuk was music to my ears and I let out a bellowing roar, welcoming Cassandra and her rhuk back.

The sky above us darkened as they swept in, each one bigger even than Cassandra. Older. Wiser. Far from useless.

Screaming defiance, they dropped toward the army, one after the other.

Once more the battle opened up, only this time there was no holding back the golems. They flowed toward us, over the dunes like an anthill kicked over and over again by a naughty child. I glanced up to see Cassandra diving into the golems and grabbing talons full of their bodies even while they hacked at her feet. She dove to the ocean and skimmed the surface, coming up with nothing but bloodied talons.

And her fellow rhuk, they were as large as her, but their feathers were dulled and many of them sported white crested necks and heads. While they moved slower than the younger rhuk, they dove and took out the golems in numbers that should pare them down rapidly.

Should.

I fought with everything I had, my eyes now solely on tossing one golem after the other into the drink. Because they were no longer trying to cut me down.

They were trying to capture me. Which meant I could draw them out to the water.

"Fen!" I yelled for him. "Grab Vahab!"

I turned and dove out into the ocean, swimming hard.

The dragon didn't hesitate but scooped up his master and then he shot toward me, dodging blows, flicking his tail at the golem that tried to grab him. He scooped me up from the ocean.

"Out, out over the water!" I clung hard to him with my paws, careful not to prick him with the tips of my claws. I did not want to hurt him, not when Lilith was a part of me.

"They're following!" Vahab shouted.

"Good. Hold your breath and dive deep!" I said, and Fen nodded. He dove straight down into the water and the first wave of the golems followed us. We floated far below the surface and watched them hit the waves, poofs of silt and clay billowing out where their bodies had been just a moment before.

But of course, we could only hold our breath for so long. Fen swam to the surface, and we bobbed up for a breath. The rhuk were making short work of the golem army and I wondered just how pissed Asag was that we'd found a way to beat him. That we'd figured out their weakness.

A few more golems tried to come at us, and we just ducked down in the waves. They would follow and turn into nothing. They didn't know that the water blew them into pieces.

I should have known the fight would not go so easily.

Less than an hour ticked by and the golems were done. I looked over my shoulder at the speck that was Lila and Reyhan. They were almost to the island by what I could see.

"Be safe, my friend," I whispered.

We made it back to the shore and I let my body shift to two legs which healed many of the wounds I'd suffered, though it depleted what was left of my reserves. I slumped to my knees and stared up at the sand dunes as my hair dripped salt water.

"Did we really just beat him?" Vahab sat next to me, elbows resting on his knees. "I mean . . . doesn't that seem a bit easy to you?"

I grimaced. "Despite how hard it was, yes. It feels . . . too easy. Which means something else?"

He nodded. "Yes, something else."

The wind whined around us, and I turned as the rhuk landed. Cassandra and a dozen others, just as she'd promised. They were covered in wounds, but nothing fatal that I could see. Cuts, bruises, a few missing feathers.

"Zamira, you saved me from the Storm Queen, and now I have saved you from Asag. We are at evens now." She bowed her head. "I wish you well."

Launching into the air, she led her other rhuk up into the sky and they fled north, away from the ocean. Away from the Storm Queen and her magic. "Thank you." I lifted my hand and bade her a silent farewell.

"Still seems too easy," Vahab muttered.

"I really wish you'd stop saying that," I shot back. "Do you want him to try again?"

"No, of course not." Vahab stood slowly, wincing, and held a hand to me. I took it and he helped pull me to my feet. "Gods, you are a solid brute, aren't you?"

I barely heard him speak. My eyes were drawn to the ocean and the frothing waves that were rolling toward us. My first thought was that we'd found a friend of the Nasnas monster.

My second was that we really should have kept our mouths shut about the ease of beating the golem army. Like ... had we learned nothing?

Apparently.

The wave slowed and washed up at our feet, and a series of eyes stared out at us. Heads slowly lifted and long hair floated on the surface of the water. I blinked a few times before I found my voice. "You don't work for Asag, do you?"

The women ducked back down, turned and slid

into the waves with a series of flips, showing off their tails. Vahab stood next to me, hands on his hips. "That was weird."

"Yeah, I don't much like it." The water stirred and frothed, as if something larger was rising from the depths, and my anxiety and adrenaline spiked hard, flooding me with the urge to grab Lilith and prepare myself.

What I didn't expect was to be grabbed from behind.

What felt like ropes dropped around me, binding my legs and arms tight to my body, before they were pulled hard at my ankles, dropping me onto my face. I yelled as I went down, and Vahab and Fen spun.

Face down in the sand, I could see nothing, and I rolled to my back.

"Aqrabuamelu," Vahab yelled. "Gods be damned, man, not you too!"

A bellowing roar rattled my innards and ears, and I found myself staring up at a body that I thought at first was a spider. No, no it was much worse than a spider.

The body of the beast was arachnid in style if you didn't count the massive curving tail that dripped with a poisonous tip. Or the body of the giant that erupted from where the scorpion's head would have been. You know, if it had been small enough to step on, and not so large that even a rhuk or a dragon would have a hard time picking it up.

I was yanked to the hands of the scorpion hybrid.

"Vahab," he bellowed. "Run while you still can."

I twisted to see Fen's face. Horror was written all over it, and then he launched himself toward us.

The arc of the scorpion's tail came down faster than I could truly follow, and then Fen was on the ground, writhing as his mouth foamed.

"NO!" I screamed the word and then more of that same sticky substance was shoved over my face and I was stuck onto the underbelly of the scorpion. Stuck. We turned and scuttled away from the ocean's edge as I thrashed, trying to get myself free.

"Do not fight me," the Aqrabuamelu said. "You will only force me to quiet you in a way you will not like."

I made myself still, but my heart and my mind raced. Fen was injured, dying.

How in the seven realms of hell was I going to get my sorry ass out of this mess?

Flying over the ocean had been a dream of mine for years—hearing the cry of the gulls, smelling the salt of the water, the glistening of waves under a bright sun. Carrying a small, writhing jungle cub while I did it? Yeah, that hadn't been in the cards I'd been looking at. "Hold still, Reyhan!"

"I am," she whimpered as she twisted in my talons for about the hundredth time.

To clarify, she was not being still.

"Almost there." I clamped my mouth shut on the flow of words that wanted to fly from me at top speed and concentrated on getting the cub to the castle. And getting back to Zam. The connection between us was there, and I could feel her shock at something. What had Vahab done this time? Or had it been Fen to surprise her? That left my heart thumping in a way that had nothing to do with my exertion. I did not want Fen to turn out that way. I wasn't sure I could do that again, you know, believe in someone's love only to have it be a total and complete lie.

Narrowing my eyes, I pushed all that away and stretched myself into the realm of exhaustion. The faster I got the cub to the Storm Queen, the better. Then I could get back to the fight and help.

The outline of the castle was clear, the rhuk resting on the battlements clearer yet. And while I could feel their eyes on us, I already knew that they would not be bothered. We were small prey to a beast that size. Small prey went unnoticed.

Ask me how I know.

Clamping my jaw tight and muttering a series of rather muddled Shakespearean curses, I prayed for a wind at the back of my wings and clutched Reyhan a little tighter.

She grumbled about being held too tight, but we were climbing now, up the side of the castle.

Better yet was a voice I knew.

"Maks!" I whispered his name to myself and angled to the left where his voice had rumbled from. He was here. I would take him with me back to Zam. We'd be together again and that may have made a tear form up in the corner of my eye.

The window where his voice came from was low down, near the water line. I doubted that would be the Storm Queen's bedroom, so maybe he hadn't been taken to her bed yet?

Only one way to find out. I flew to the window, the bars keeping me from going in. Carefully I landed and pinned Reyhan between me and the bars, only to have her slip through. Damn cats and their rubber bodies!

"Reyhan!" I reached for her as she fell, but she was caught by a set of hands.

"Lila?" Maks stood and we were eye level. Reyhan curled in his arms, purring.

"You smell like Zam," she said.

He looked at her and then to me. "Lila, what are you doing here? Where's Zam?"

I opened my mouth and then noticed the chains on his wrists. Prisoner, was he? "Long story, let me sum up. Zam might be in trouble. We need the magic thingy from here. Then we need to go back to Zam." I pointed with the tips of my claws as I spoke, from him, to the castle, then back the way we'd come.

"And what about me?" Reyhan asked.

I motioned for Maks to come closer and I gripped his face with my claws. "The demon wants the kid. Mamitu said the girl would be safe here."

Maks shook his head. "I wouldn't leave her here. Not with Dani."

My eyebrows shot up and anger on Zam's behalf shot up with them. "First-name basis, huh? Do you call her honey too?"

Maks stared hard at me, his blue eyes never wavering. "If I lose my honor, I lose myself."

Tension flowed out of me and I let out a long sigh.

"Antony and Cleopatra, as if you could stump me. And you're damn lucky you didn't lose your honor. I'd have made sure you lost what you lost your honor on." I glanced at his crotch, to make sure he got the point. Then pointed to make doubly sure.

He smiled, but it wasn't a happy smile. More like a tired one. "It came close."

That was not what I wanted to hear, but at least he'd kept his pants on. "Hold your wrists up." He did as I asked and I brought up a little acid, spitting it on the chains that were holding him prisoner. I mean, I wasn't so pissed that I would spit right on the manacles.

The acid ate through the chains in seconds. He rubbed his wrists. "The door is locked too."

"I gotta do everything around here," I muttered. "Hang on to Reyhan. I'll get you out."

I leaned out on the ledge, looking for another window. There was one about five feet to my right. Close enough; it should be to the room leading into Maks's cell.

I snorted. *Of course* he'd gotten himself caught, chained, and stuck. It seemed that as much trouble as Zam found, Maks found just as much, and I was always bailing them out. I smiled to myself, flew to the window and slid through. No bars on this one. I blinked in the change of light.

"Who be you?"

I spun and let out a roar as someone grabbed my tail.

"Oh, a tiny roar even!" A cackle came next and I yanked my tail out of the hands of a very old, very frail looking woman. The thing was, she smelled like a Jinn. I wrinkled my nose.

"I'm here for my friend."

"Good, I'm tired of watching him." She waved a hand at me, turned and left. But not before she flipped a key over her shoulder. "I'd hurry, if you want to get him out of here before Dani realizes he's gone . . . she still has some hope that he might give her a child. Foolish girl."

Foolish indeed.

I dropped down, scooped the key up and jammed it into the locked door. Maks stepped out and looked around. "Where is the old woman? I was sure I heard her."

"You did; she left and told us to hurry."

Maks still held Reyhan tucked under his arm. "You got a plan to get off the island?"

"Of course." I most certainly did not, but he didn't have to know that. "First we have to get the source of magic. We need that."

He gave a quick nod. "That we can do. Come on."

In a blink, he'd shifted to his caracal form and he and Reyhan padded along the stone floors, me following just above their heads.

Maks led us through the castle, heading further down. I didn't think it was possible, but we were surely below the water level by the time he came to a stop.

"Here." He pointed with his nose at a small circle of water that was glowing slightly. I didn't like it, didn't like the look of it at all, but before I could say anything Maks was speaking. "I'll dive through and grab it; you guard the hole."

He shifted back to two legs and then dove into the narrow circular bit of water, disappearing with barely a splash.

"Idiot!" I hissed at him as I flipped and rolled in the air, my guts twisted up. "Maks, you get back here right now!"

The thing was, I didn't hear the door behind me, or smell them until it was much, much too late.

A band of magic wrapped around me, pinning my wings to my sides and dropping me to the ground. I twisted around to see a woman with long, wild dark hair and deep green eyes looking down at me. She also smelled like a Jinn.

"Run, Reyhan!" I yelled as I twisted around, trying to get close enough to spit acid on the Storm Queen's feet.

Reyhan bolted from the room, but the Storm Queen never even looked at her. "You, you are the one I want. The prophecy has changed," she purred. "And you will be my weapon to kill Asag."

I roared at her and hoped to hell that Maks could hear me.

"Parting is such sweet sorrow!" I bellowed the words out, the quickest thing I could come up with.

The Storm Queen reached down and grabbed me by the tail, holding me up so she could inspect me. "I've never captured a dragon before." Her smile was slow and spread wide across her face. "What a boon that you came to me. Mamitu was right. The time is now for me."

"Listen, you can't be serious about taking me to Asag!" I yelled at the giant scorpion man who had me clutched tightly. "You can't tell me that you like Asag!" I was frantic. Trying to figure out just how the hell I was going to get away from the Aqrabuamelu—or scorpion man if you prefer. Huge didn't even begin to cover it. He was as big as any giant I'd ever dealt with. Possibly bigger.

Let me help you.

I grimaced. "Come on, I really don't want to kill you!"

That stopped him and he twisted around and under his belly to look at me. Even though his upper body was technically human, it was oversized. He looked like a giant had been cut in half and stuck on top of a giant scorpion.

"You can't kill me."

"Wanna bet?" I threw out. Because if Asag wanted me, I'd rather he took me in pieces if I had to choose a way to show up on his doorstep.

Lilith shivered against my back. She'd been a flail when I'd stuck her there, but she began to shift until she was far slimmer. A spear? She slid down into my hands, the metal rod the perfect width for my palm.

The scorpion man tipped his head sideways. "No one likes Asag, but he rules our world and does so with no mercy. So, I suggest you get used to the idea."

"What if I told you I was going to kill him?" I offered. The hold on me tightened and I struggled to breathe. Spots danced in my vision and even though I could have spun Lilith and jabbed her into his back, I hesitated.

At the edge of the darkness, my hand tensed and the Aqrabuamelu loosened his hold on me. He didn't let go, just . . . eased off. "You."

I coughed. "Me."

He drew me up until we were eye to eye. "How?"

In for a penny, in for all the pounds. "I am following the stupid rules, working on the second challenge, and I have Lilith. I have a black horse, a dragon, and I think all the other pieces that need to be in place. I'm close."

Was I rambling? Yup, because his stinger was hovering just behind his head, ready to stab me. The drop of venom on the tip was more than freaking me out. He tore me away from his belly with his clawed hand and held me up so that I was right in his face. He didn't smell bad, but this close to his mouth where he could stuff me in with one bite was far from comforting.

"You are not lying." He seemed surprised, and he touched his face, rubbing at his chin.

"No. I'm not. You want me to?" I wasn't sure where this was going. I was hoping he'd let me go. That's all I had left.

Hope.

And a demon blade strapped to my back.

"I cannot turn away from the task handed to me," he said, deep gray eyes narrowing in thought. "But I can offer you a . . . possibility. Since you obviously like to take chances." He leaned down to the sand and shoved his hand into it, rooting around a moment, and came up with a handful of sand, as far as I could see.

He sprinkled it over my head; I closed my eyes as the sand trickled over me. Only the trickling sand turned to tickling feet. My eyes flew open as the deadly scorpion crawled over my shoulder and settled against my chest.

The Aqrabuamelu blew a lungful of air at me, and the scorpion cracked in half, twisting around until its body became the links of a necklace, its stinger the pendant in the middle.

"I don't need—"

"You have until the sun touches the horizon. Whoever wears the necklace when the light leaves the sky, will be brought back here to me. Perhaps that will be you. Perhaps that will be someone you convince to take the necklace off, for you cannot."

A chance. Not a great chance, but it was a chance I'd take. "Done."

His smile seemed genuine, which bothered me. The monsters were not supposed to be . . . the nice ones.

"My name is—"

"Please don't say Steve," I said on nothing but instinct.

His eyebrows shot up and my guts clenched. I didn't think I could handle another Steve in my life. "It is not Steve."

I sighed.

"But you are close, it is Steven." He gave a low sigh and if I could have groaned, I would have. "I am a fool for hoping you have a chance. But I am going to give it to you. I am a guardian of the desert, and I have been stymied by the demon. He has done much harm, and I do not know that it could ever be reversed." His hold tightened on me until I could not take a breath. "I will let you go, because I hear the truth in you. But know this."

I was pretty sure my ribs were cracking.

"If you think to try and fool me, and are not horribly destroyed by the demon, I will kill you."

As quickly as he'd scooped me up, he dropped me into the sand. His massive body scuttled above me, and I lay there, just trying to catch my wind. "I hope he doesn't kill you!" I mean, he wasn't a Steve—not really.

"I will wait here until the night comes and you, or another, is brought back to me. I suggest you hurry yourself along," Steven called to me over his back, his tail bobbing far above his head giving me the shivers. Then his words sunk in.

Fuck. I had to get to the Storm Queen still.

And I had to do it in a goddess-damned hurry.

I scrambled up, one hand still clutching Lilith in her new form. Spinning around, I ran back toward the beach. Fen had been hurt bad by the sting of Steven, and who knew what Vahab had done to help him. If anything.

The long spear that was now Lilith was light, at least—a boon in all her forms. There was not much weight to a magical weapon in my experience. Which was good. Because I was fucking done, exhausted and couldn't take many more hits.

I was sliding down the last dune toward the water, heading straight toward the far too still form of Fen, before I saw that Vahab was nowhere to be seen.

"Fen, I'm coming!" I yelled. I ran past my saddle-bags that had been trampled heavily, scooped them up and kept on running. I dropped to my knees next to Fen and dug around in the bags until I found the unicorn horn.

I put a hand to Fen's head. "Fen, you have to wake up." The poison was heavy in him, and his body was far too cool for anything good.

Nothing, no heartbeat.

I slid my hand down his neck, looking for a pulse, something to tell me I wasn't too late. All I could think was that Lila would be devastated if . . . no. I couldn't let it happen. I clutched the horn, thinking that it wasn't supposed to be this way.

There, under my left hand was a flutter, just the smallest thump. Good enough. I pressed the tip of the horn to Fen's side and breathed out as the horn lit up, glowing bright for a second before that glow slid from the base all the way to the tip and into Fen's body.

The dragon gave a gasping lurch and rolled to his feet, albeit shaking and dripping with sweat.

Sweat? Dragons didn't sweat.

"Fen?"

"Too much of the golems' poison and the scorpion," he said through chattering teeth, his body trembling top to bottom as the poison dripped out of him, sizzling as it hit the sand around him, turning it into bits of glass. All of it chased out by the magic of the horn. I looked at said horn in my hand and nearly dropped it.

No longer pristine white, half the horn was darkening to a charcoal gray right before my eyes, with only the top third still the original shimmering white. I tucked it into the saddlebags. There was nothing I could do for it now, and I wouldn't regret saving a life when I could.

Fen slowly turned his head to me. "Vahab left me."

"He thought you were dead." I spun Lilith and

strapped her to my back once more. She hadn't even tried to get me to kill Fen. Interesting.

"No, I was still talking to him." Fen frowned, and his lips pulled back from his teeth. "That prick left me to die alone. He's swimming across to get to the Jinn woman."

I lifted both hands, palms up. "He's not a good guy. Are you just realizing this?"

Fen snapped his teeth once. "The bonds between us were broken, he freed me."

"Is that good?"

He butted his head against me. "It means I can come with you and Lila, wherever you go until—"

I put a hand on his mane, digging my fingers into it. "No time for that now. You got it in you to fly?"

He lifted his head sharply and flipped me onto his back. "We going to the Storm Queen? That's where Lila is."

"You bet your sweet ass," I said. "One needs a serious ass whooping and I am just the shifter to give it to her. The other needs you to love her with every beat of your heart. And we have to do it all before the sun is gone." I looked to the sky. We didn't have a lot of time. An hour if I was lucky.

He twisted around and looked at me. "And if she hates me?"

I winked at him. "She does not hate you. Trust me on this."

He gave me a quick nod and then leapt into the sky,

his body undulating as he picked up speed. I buried my hands in his mane and looked out across the water toward the Storm Queen's keep.

The waves were thrashing and as we drew close, I could easily see the rhuk waiting, then rising into the sky as they took us in as a threat.

"Fen, we gotta take the small route. I'll shift first, then you shift and grab me." This was a moment of ultimate trust. Because if he didn't grab me, I was hitting the water and had a hell of a long swim in waters that were likely less than friendly.

Even as I thought it a long tentacle reached for us, flopping back when it fell short. Fuck, that was not something I wanted to tangle with. Not one damn bit.

I breathed out and stepped between the doorway in my mind, shifting into a small house cat.

At the same time Fen shifted under me, and I fell holding my breath, legs wide to slow my descent until a set of talons dug into me, stopping my free fall.

"Got ya," he grunted as we continued on toward the keep.

"Thanks. I did not want to go swimming."

"Lila would kill me if I let you get hurt," he said.

"She would. And then she might just bring you back to life, and kill you again to make sure."

He laughed. "Somehow I don't doubt it."

I looked ahead to see the rhuk settling back down. The threat, aka the large green and white dragon, was gone in their eyes.

"What fools these mortals be," I whispered. "Fen, head for the rooftop over there."

Set on the southern side of the castle, it was flat and didn't look to be guarded by anyone or anything—rhuk included.

Fen brought us down carefully and let me go so I could leap out of his hands. I shifted so that as I landed, I did so on two feet in a crouch. "Lilith, I'm going to pull you around. Do not fuck with me."

I will be on my best behavior.

Call me crazy, but I doubted that. I crept forward, motioning for Fen to join me. He swept up to my shoulders and looped himself around my neck the way Lila did. "Will she be mad?"

"She's going to be right pissed that we slipped in undetected," I muttered as I made my way across the open space to the only door leading onto the upper rooftop.

"No, I meant Lila. That I'm in her spot."

"Stop overthinking things, Fen," I muttered as I put my hand to the door and let myself in.

Into the lion's den.

Good thing I'd grown up in a pride of lions and knew just where to strike the underbelly.

Maks did not leap out of the water—I'd more than half expected him to come out and kick the Storm Queen's ass. But who was I kidding? He'd had his powers stripped the same as me and Zam. If he could have done it, he would have already.

Speaking of . . . the Storm Queen spun me around, holding me by my tail. "Come now, you must have a name?"

I grimaced, debating if it mattered. "How about a whole sandbox of fuck off with you?"

She smiled. "I am Dani. And you will obey me."

I did not like the sound of that. I liked it even less as the tendrils of her magic dug through my body, into my muscles and bones. I bared my teeth at her again.

"Oh, that is interesting. Asag has taken some abilities from you?" She sucked a breath in slowly. "Very interesting. You have abilities with weather?"

I did, because I'd taken them from another dragon, just like my father had the ability to do. I snapped my teeth at her, even though she was out of range. It was all I had left to me.

Her hand shot at my neck, and she snagged me tight, her magic digging in further. "Yes, very interesting. I see why he took all your abilities and power. You have much in you to frighten him."

I wanted to growl, to bite her fingers off one at a time, to claw her eyes out. But I had nothing. Dani put me down and the hold on me was gone. Only I didn't have any way to move on my own. She snapped her fingers and pointed to her shoulder.

My body was not my own.

I leapt up and flew to her shoulder, perching myself there. Wrapping my tail lightly around her neck for balance.

"There, that is better."

"I hate the murdered, love him murdered," I spit at her.

"Are you speaking in tongues now? Another gift?"

I couldn't even dig my claws in more than she would allow. "A fool thinks himself to be wise, but a wise man knows himself to be a fool."

The slap came unexpected and rang my bell hard and left my ears ringing. I blinked away tears—not from the pain, it wasn't bad—but the sheer suddenness of the blow.

"I am no fool, and you'd best remember that if you wish to keep your pretty indigo hide intact."

I wasn't sure she knew who she was dealing with. Strike that; she had no idea, and that made her a fool to not know her enemy.

"Zam is going to wipe the floor with you," I growled. "Like the dirty rag you are."

The Storm Queen snapped her fingers and my mouth clamped shut, muscles spasming and grinding my teeth together until true tears did form.

She swept out of the tiny, cold dank room, and up the stairs. I glanced back once, but still didn't see Maks.

He couldn't have been under the water that long and survive, and I couldn't even go after him. My heart cracked. We couldn't lose Toad, not when we'd come so far. Not when we were so close. I closed my eyes and cried for him, just for a moment.

Because there was no time. Zam would still come for him, not knowing he was gone. She would come for me and Reyhan.

And I had to be ready to help her.

A deal with a scorpion hybrid was perhaps one of the best and worst ideas I'd ever had, and I couldn't help but check the height of the sun at each window. The scorpion stinger that hung on a thread around my neck bumped me here and there, giving a tickle, reminding me that I had to hurry my ass up. And that I needed someone else to take it off me.

I could feel Lila, Maks and Reyhan, but none of them were in the same place. I let out a low growl just as my ears picked up footsteps.

Ducking into a side alcove, I pulled my cloak around me and Fen and shrunk back into the shadows as best I could. The fighting would come, I wasn't worried about that. I just wanted to get to the Storm Queen before it happened.

But where was she? Did she have one of my friends?

Fuck, she probably had Maks. Which made my blood boil. Lila was pissed, that much was coming through loud and clear; Reyhan was—shocker—sleeping.

From what I could tell, Maks was deep in the castle, far below me. At the rate I was running into guards and other people, I was going to run out of time. Which meant I would be yanked back to my new friend Steven.

Yeah, that was not the goal.

Time to get tiny. I shifted to my house cat form and scooted forward, still using the shadows but moving a hell of a lot quicker. The guards didn't so much as blink as I ran between their legs, bounced off walls and raced downstairs. Following Maks's threads, I leapt down a final set of stairs and landed in front of a door. A door and a very old lady.

She was frail, that was the only word I could fathom for her. Thin, reed-like, white hair that was wild as if windswept. Her eyes landed on me, and I immediately cringed, my hair standing up all over my body.

"Who are you?" She pointed a finger at me, and I cringed further, trying to play up like I really was just a cat. Above my head, crawling across the ceiling above her Fen moved silently. He lifted his eyebrows, and I shook my head. I didn't know this woman. She might be a maid. Hell, for all I knew she was the Storm Queen.

That thought took hold and I let out a long low hiss.

No wonder she was having difficulty getting pregnant. Her eggs should have been all dried up by her age.

Her frown slowly turned into a smile. "Ah, you must be his mate? He is in there. Dive into the water if you wish to find him."

And then she turned and opened the door, waving for me to go in. A trick? Maybe, but I could feel Maks on the other side of the door and she didn't know that. I scuttled through and Fen followed, staying just out of sight of the woman. She shut the door behind me.

"Forgive me."

Fuck, was that for me? She'd whispered the two words. I stepped through the doorway in my mind, shifting back to two legs. The space was circular, with a pool of water in front of me. Little lights flickered in the water, and I stared into it. I could swim, but let's be honest, I was a desert girl through and through. The idea of diving into a tunnel of water with no way to know how deep it was, or if there was a place to come out . . . it gave me more than a little pause.

Cold, clammy sweat broke out across my body. "Fen, what do you think?"

I could feel Maks there, below me still. Somewhere in the water. He wasn't dead. And he wasn't scared. How long had he been there?

"You're sure he's . . . in there?" Fen dropped to my shoulder. "If you're sure, then you dive in."

He was right about that. "You coming with me?"

"Yes, I think that's best." His tightened his hold

around my neck, just to the point of being uncomfortable. "I feel a pull to this place too."

I stripped out of my clothes, down to my bare skin, and then I hesitated as I laid Lilith on the floor.

Bad idea.

"So many of them are," I muttered. The thing was I needed to be able to swim, and packing clothes and weapons was not going to help me.

I stood at the edge of the pool. The water lapped up over my toes, just warm enough to make it feel as though I would be stepping into air and not water.

Lifting a foot, I stepped out over the pool and let my body sink down, taking a deep breath as I went.

The water closed over my head without so much as a single wave. Spinning, I turned and began to swim down, toward the pull that was Maks. That was my only option now. Swim hard and pray to whatever gods would listen that I would make it.

Fear—at turns hot and cold—drove me and I could feel the air running out in my lungs. Crap, where was Maks?

As my legs and arms began to burn in earnest, as I began to think I needed to turn around, there was a glimmer of something ahead of me. Something impossible.

A beach?

I didn't question what I was seeing, I didn't have enough oxygen to dilly-dally. I swam with all I had, Fen using his tail as a propellor helping us along. My fingers reached for the sand as I drew close and the world turned upside down, and I was spat out onto a sandy beach. Coughing, I spat out a mouthful of water and then drew in a deep breath.

"Okay, this is weird," Fen whispered. "How are we . . . not in water anymore?"

"Yeah, I don't know." I pushed to my feet and looked at the sand around us. There was a set of footprints leading up the beach, away from the water and into the trees surrounding the edge. I looked over my shoulder at the dark water that waited out there.

Shivering, I took off after the footsteps.

"You sure you should run? Your bits are bouncing," Fen said.

"Really?" I muttered. "They aren't even that big."

"Just thinking it looks painful," he grumbled and then leapt off my shoulder to fly ahead of me.

I kept on jogging. I wasn't quite ready to call for Maks, just in case, well, in case he didn't answer. I'd learned that sometimes the bonds between me and my family could be strange.

The land angled upward, and I reached the top in a matter of seconds only to find myself staring down at Maks crouched over something.

"Maks!"

He didn't turn around. Not once.

Fen flew around his head. "Is this him? His face is stuck in something!"

Stuck in something? Well, at least it wasn't someone else's lady parts.

I reached Maks and put a hand to his back as I stepped around to face him. His head was bowed over what I first thought was a bowl, and then realized was a crystalline diamond. No, not a diamond.

"This is it, the source of all magic."

I pulled Maks back and he came away from the diamond, gasping as if coming up for air.

"It's what?" Fen barked. "What did you say?"

I knelt next to Maks, turning his face to me. "Maks, are you okay?"

He blinked, blue eyes uncertain for a moment, and then he scrambled away from me. "Fuck off, Dani."

My hands were empty and my eyebrows were high. "Who the fuck is Dani?"

He narrowed his eyes at me, and though he seemed calm I could see the distinct rapid beat of his heart in his throat. "Zam?"

What had happened? He thought I was someone else? "Who is Dani?"

"She is the Storm Queen." He stared hard at me. "You aren't her?"

"What happened?"

He all but crawled toward me, scooping me into his arms, burying his face in the crook of my neck. "Zam, Zam, Zam." Just my name, over and over as he clung to me. I held him tight, not really sure what else to do. But we were together and that meant we could do this.

Hope is a funny thing, you know; sometimes it shows up when you don't even know you needed it.

"I'm here now."

His hands traced my back, and then I realized he was tracing my scars. "This is how I knew it wasn't you. She made herself look like you, but there were no scars." He kissed one that lay across my shoulder. "Your scars are what saved me."

I leaned back. "No matter what happened, you survived. That's what's important, Maks. I don't care what happened."

He cupped my face. "But I do. And nothing happened. It . . . came close. She made herself look like you and gave me something . . . it was not good. But I touched a scar, and it wasn't there. There were no scars."

Drawing my face close, he kissed me gently. His emotions came through the kiss loud and clear, and I returned them, knowing we didn't have time but wanting to take the moment. Letting myself breathe him in while we had a chance. Time was ticking, I could feel it in the pressure of the stinger against my neck.

I forced myself to pull back. "Maks, we have to go." I scooped up the diamond, the source of all magic. It was big, far too big to be packing around. "And we have to take this."

Fen dropped from the sky. "How are you going to do that?"

"Lila?" Maks stared at the very obviously not Lila dragon. "Who are you?"

"This is Fen, Lila loves him, so be nice."

Fen shot a look at me. "Are you . . . you think she does?"

"Pretty sure." I didn't look at him as I rolled the source of all magic in my hands. I mean, for being that, it didn't give off even a vibe of power. "Did you break it?"

"I did not break it," Maks said. "You have to stick your face into the water in the chalice and then it shows you what I think is a potential future. I think. For all I know it could be total and complete lies." He frowned as if . . .

"What did you see?"

He shook his head. "No. I don't even want to say it out loud. The things I saw, if they are true . . . or they might come to pass, I don't want—" He rubbed his hand over his face.

"So it gave you a clue to the future?"

"Possible future, though I don't think that's actually what it's for. I mean, if it's the source of all magic, I guess it can do whatever it wants." He spoke as if it was alive. Like the source of all magic was a living, breathing creature.

And that felt . . . right.

I ran my hands over it, feeling the edges. "No, I don't think this is it. Shouldn't that feel like something important? Powerful? But maybe this," I rolled the diamond thing over in my hands, the sparkling water sloshing, "is a distraction?"

Fen dropped not to my shoulder, but to Maks's. "Like a false lead?"

I nodded. "Anyone coming here would look at this and think it's the source of magic. Or at the very least something worth taking."

Before I could change my mind, I plunged my face into the water of the chalice, a question on my lips. Where was the source of magic?

Like dreaming, I stared at the bottom of the chalice, eyes wide open as the water swirled.

Alive. Living.

Breathe the magic in, someone whispered. *Take it into you.*

I didn't hesitate but sucked in a lungful of the water. It didn't burn, it didn't feel like I was drowning.

No, I was being filled up, more alive than I'd ever been. Colors danced and sparkled across my vision, and I saw what I had to do in those moments. How to make things right.

I slowly lifted my head and I knew that Maks had been onto it. Lilith had helped me put it in play.

"What is life in the desert?" I asked.

"Water," Fen and Maks answered together.

Maks stared at me. "It's in you. You drank it in?" Not a question, a statement.

"Breathed. Now let's go." I clutched at the chalice, dragging it with me.

"Leave it." Maks tried to take it from me, and I shook my head.

"It'll make a great distraction. Anyone who has seen it thinks the chalice is the key, not the liquid."

He took my other hand, and we ran up the slope, through the oasis and down the sandy beach to the strange ocean. We dove in side by side, and the world flipped upside down. Together we swam for the surface, Maks just ahead of me.

But against my chest, the scorpion sting shifted, scratching at me. Shit.

We were almost out of time.

I yanked my clothes back on—not an easy feat over a damp body—and quickly strapped Lilith to my back.

What is this? Something has possessed you!

"Not exactly." I wasn't going to try and explain to her that the source of magic needed a vessel. Already I could feel the drain on my reserves. I had to get out of here and to Pazuzu as fast as I could. I needed it out of me.

"We get Lila, Reyhan, and we go," Maks said. "We aren't strong enough to face the Storm Queen."

For once I didn't argue. I just nodded. "Agreed. Fen, can you find Reyhan? Bring her to the top tower, we'll leave from there." Inside my head I found the thread that was little Reyhan—still sleeping—and tied them to the threads that were Fen. "Okay?"

He shook his head, white mane flipping around. "Yeah, I got her. Go."

Maks put a hand under my elbow. "Zam, are you okay?"

I gave him a quick nod. "I am. We just have to go. We have until sunset and that is not far off."

Lilith was muttering in a continuous stream under her breath, but I ignored her. I shouldn't have, but I did.

There was no way I was about to tell him that I could feel the magic eating away at me. This was why it was in a diamond chalice—something strong enough to hold all that power. I tightened my grip on said chalice. This was my hail Mary, as my dad had been fond of saying. What a woman named Mary had to do with a last chance was beyond me, but he said it and I believed him.

"The top tower is above Dani's bedroom," Maks said.

I fought the spurt of jealousy, knowing that he'd fended her off still had me wanting to kick her in the lady parts. Because I was certainly no lady, I said fuck, and had no problem going to war for my mate.

"Stop growling, Zam," Maks said softly; "guards up ahead."

I bit my tongue until I tasted blood to still the sounds rippling out of my mouth. I couldn't help it. Maks was mine, and I'd worked too damn hard to get him to lose him to some hussy with more magic than me.

Up and up, we went, using the various staircases, always following the pull toward Lila. Where was she? Hiding in a crevice somewhere, most likely. Or snooping to find some new brand of liquor she could thieve.

"No guards," I pointed out as we climbed the fourth set of stairs. "No people at all."

Maks slowed. "Did anyone see you and Fen when you slipped in?"

"An old woman."

He groaned. "White crazy hair?"

That he knew exactly who I was talking about did not bode well. "Why?"

"That's Dani's grandmother. If she knew you were here..."

A shuffle in the hall to our left turned us both. There she was, the old lady in question. "Then I might tell my granddaughter that you are here for your mate? Perhaps. Perhaps. Or maybe I know that the best way to deal with Asag is not through the death of my last family member. Perhaps I wish it to be someone else, and I would do all I can to make sure that she," the old woman pointed a bent stick at me, "is the one to take my Dani's place."

"You'll help us escape?" Maks said. "For real this time, Arin?"

"I needed your mate to come for you," the old woman—Arin, apparently—said. "I needed her to take the chalice and complete the next step. My Dani is not the one for Asag. She never understood . . . well, anything. I am here on her sufferance if you have not noticed. She'd kill me if I got in her way too, Jinn."

I wasn't about to tell her that was exactly what I was going to do—give little Dani a piece of her own medicine. But maybe Arin wouldn't care.

Arin made a shooing motion. "I have made sure that the guards are in the mess hall. Dani sleeps. Go."

We turned and ran. This was our chance. Near the top of the castle, Fen caught up to us, Reyhan in his talons. She let out a big yawn and reached for me with her paws. Maks scooped her into his arms, and we kept on moving. The upside of all this? Lila was close, I could feel her.

"We get Lila and we go," I said quietly, then motioned to Fen with one hand. "Can you carry all of us?"

"Not for a long distance, but to the shore I can do it. What about the rhuk?"

"We'll go fast and hard; stay closer to the water and hope that they take their time," Fen said. "It's all we can do."

Not much of a plan, but like Fen said, there wasn't much else we could do.

At the top of the last stairs was a single door and Maks slowed, his mouth moving but the words barely above a whisper. "Storm Queen."

And Lila was in there. Of all the places for her to hide, why did it have to be in there?

I took a shaky breath and put a hand on the door, pushing it open, praying there were no creaking hinges.

Maks touched my arm, stepped around me and took the lead, holding Reyhan under one arm. I followed him through. Fen stayed up on the ceiling, just watching.

The room was dark and smelled like a heavy cloying perfume despite the breeze blowing in off the rooftop, through the far open door.

I moved to the left, feeling Lila there.

But someone stepped out in front of us, blocking our path.

The Storm Queen strode out of the shadows, barely dressed. Her outfit was transparent, and where it wasn't transparent, it just wasn't even there. "So, lover, you decided to bring your pet to me? Lovely, I knew I could count on you."

I didn't know who she was referring to, me or Reyhan.

No, she wasn't looking at me, but at the cub.

Maybe thinking she was . . . a small black house cat.

Her hand lifted, electricity dancing around her fingers. Nope, that couldn't happen.

"Over here, you bawling, blasphemous incharitable bitch!" I held up the chalice. "You want it?"

She turned to me, eyes widening and then snapping into a laser beam focus. "That is mine."

"Is it?" I turned it over in my hands, shrugged and threw it to her.

She screeched and dove for it as I dove for her. What I didn't expect was the claws on the back of my head, yanking my hair and pulling me off course.

I spun, saw Lila's scales and understood immediately. She'd been taken like the rhuk were taken.

"Stealing my friends?" I snarled. "Fen, take Lila out, and watch her mouth."

"On it!"

I rolled to my hands and knees, eye to eye with the Storm Queen. "You and I need to have a chat."

That was not what he'd have thought Zam would say to Dani. A chat? Then again, Zam had a funny way of putting things. Yeah, a chat was not what his mate meant at all. She launched herself at the Storm Queen and they rolled across the floor. Dani let out a screech and a bolt of electricity ripped out of her, just missing Zam.

Outside the sun was dipping low.

What had Zam said? Sunset was key. He dropped Reyhan. "Stay out of the way, kid."

She let out a startled yowl but hit the ground on all fours. Maks leapt into the fray as Zam knelt over Dani and was delivering blow after blow to the Storm Queen's face. Dani's magic flowed around them, but didn't seem to be hitting Zam. He didn't know why and didn't care. He just knew that at least for now they had the upper hand.

Dani was howling, Zam was letting off a streaming flow of curses, Fen yelped and fell to the ground, then Lila was there, clawing at Zam again.

Tears flowed down Lila's face as she attacked her friend.

Maks did the only thing he could. He grabbed Lila by the tail and then pinned her wings to her sides. "Lila, you have to fight her power! You have to!"

She let out a tiny roar. A snarl and then she closed her eyes, tears still falling. Maybe that was all she had left to her in her control.

"I've got her arms, I need to . . . fuck the sun!" Zam cried out and she shook her head. "The scorpion stinger, it needs to be on her! I need someone else to take it off!"

He looked around. He couldn't let go of Lila. Fen was wobbling across the floor, unbalanced from his fight with Lila. "The kid!"

"Reyhan!" Zam yelled. "To me!"

The cub bounded across to Zam and shifted to two feet, wobbling a little. "What do you want me to do?"

Dani groaned, eyes closed, hurt and momentarily not throwing her weight around, but he could see the strain in Zam's arms as she held the Storm Queen tight.

"Take my necklace off," Zam gritted out the words. "Hurry."

She bowed her head as Reyhan slid the necklace off. And then put it over her own head. "Like this?"

"No!" Zam cried out and the kid startled backward.

"No, take it off, put it on the woman here!"

Reyhan frowned. "But I like it. It's pretty."

Zam's entire body was shaking as she kept Dani's hands pinned. He fought with the still-writhing dragon in his hands, unable to loosen his hold. "Listen to me, Reyhan." Zam's eyes shot to the sun going down. "Put it on the woman here. Now. Please!"

Reyhan frowned and pouted, her hands going to the necklace.

As the light of the day disappeared, she began to lift it off her neck toward Zam as Maks continued to wrestle with Lila. "Fine!"

"Fen, help her!" Zam yelled and the white maned dragon shot to Reyhan, clinging to her back.

Too slow, it was too slow.

A blinding light filled the air, the glow coming off the necklace, and the stinger seemed to come alive. It shot toward Reyhan's chest, driving in deep, a trail of blood sliding down her shirt. She cried out and her eyes went to Zam's.

"I'm sorry, I should have listened better."

Zam let go of Dani and reached for Reyhan, but her fingers went through the empty space where the kid and Fen had been just a moment before. A howl poured out of his mate's mouth, one that turned into the roar of a mother lion losing a cub. Her whole body shook as she clutched at the space where Reyhan had been.

And there wasn't a damn thing he could do about it.

Dani groaned and opened her eyes, but her hands were already lifting, crackling with power. A spell woven of death and pain, she flicked her fingers at Zam.

Keeping Lila tucked under one arm, he leapt forward and tackled his mate, taking her down and away from the Storm Queen. The magic shot over their heads, slamming into the wall behind them.

Zam spun out from under him, stood and pulled a weapon he didn't recognize. A long spear with an edged blade on one end. More than that, though, what caught his attention was the look in her eyes.

As if it was not Zam he was seeing, but someone else—her eyes were deep red. She spun the pole arm toward Dani, not hesitating, not for even a hairsbreadth.

Dani barely dodged the first swing. Maks still had Lila pinned under him and she was squirming to get out.

"I'm good, I'm good!" Lila screamed. "Let me help!"

He wasn't sure that he could trust her, not when she'd been so obviously captured by Dani. But he let her go.

Lila flew up and went straight to Zam, wrapping herself around her shoulders. "Oh shit, Maks! This is bad!"

"How can it get worse?" He rolled to his feet and took a stance between the two women. Not that he was trying to protect Dani. Not at all. He just wasn't sure who was in charge of Zam's body right then.

L ilith had me in her hold completely. I could feel my body moving, could feel her directing my limbs. "That's right, Storm Queen. You're going to die," I purred. "I can see the knowing in your eyes."

Dani snarled and flicked her hands at me. I spun the pole arm, catching the spell, wrapping it around the weapon and then flinging it back at her.

She screamed and dove to the side, taking her out the door to the upper rooftop. I followed, though saying I followed was not correct. Lilith followed her while I fought desperately for control of my own body.

"I am running things now," my voice said, and I knew that Lilith did not mean that for Dani. It was for me.

You've been laying low. Making me believe you really

want to help. Now it was my voice that was inside my head.

Her laugh was sharp and hard. "See, you are not so stupid after all. I am a *demon,* you idiot. I have no interest in anything but my own designs. And with you so graciously taking the source of all magic into you, I knew it was time to make my move. That is enough power for me to rule the world with. I can go straight to Asag. That is the beauty for me—I don't have to follow the rules."

"You did what?" Dani screamed. "You can't! You can't take it, that's the only thing keeping Asag at bay!"

Lilith swung the weapon at Dani again, almost sloppy in her movements. Then again, it wasn't like she'd had a body for a long time.

What were my options? I thought through my limited options while Dani and Lilith fought. There was screaming and then a thud. I had to make my move.

I reached for my connection to Lila who I could feel on my shoulders. *Pain had disrupted her before. I need you to hurt me.*

Lila growled. "I don't want to."

You must.

I couldn't feel anything, but by the screeching coming out of my mouth, Lila was clawing the shit out of me. Lilith. Whatever.

There was a moment where the pain broke through

and I took a deep breath, took hold of my alpha power and grasped the reins of my body. I stumbled back and stared down at the body of Dani.

She'd been cut to pieces. Literally.

Head, legs, and arms had been sliced off.

Lilith surged in me, and I snarled. "Not today, demon."

I went to my hands and knees, fighting off her attempts to control me. And when that didn't work, she did something I didn't think was possible.

She pulled me into the dreamscape.

My body fell to the stone rooftop, Maks was hollering, Lila screamed my name and then I was standing on the roof facing a woman I'd never seen before, but I would have recognized her anywhere.

Her hair was blood-red, and her eyes matched that impossible color. Her body was sleek, and she sported a small pair of mottled red wings. Two sets of arms sprouted from her sides. She put one set on her hips and the other she folded.

"So it has come to this. Winner takes all." She smiled, showing off only four very sharp pointed teeth.

I stared at her. "You were always lying to me."

"Darling," she laughed. "Don't be so surprised. I'm a demon, it's what I do. It's what I live for." Her smile widened.

And before I could take another breath, she launched herself at me, all four arms reaching for me.

As if I would just lie down and let her take my life.

Fuck her and her stupidity.

I kicked the left bottom wrist, snapping the bones, spun low and grabbed the right bottom arm. I kept on turning, twisting the arm around and up behind her, angling it for a clean break. She howled and tried to follow me.

"You forget," I snarled as I jerked her arm hard, cracking it right at the elbow. "I'm a shifter, a Jinn, and a little bit dragon. Which makes me mean as fuck when it comes to fighting. Weapons or no weapons."

She twisted around, bottom two arms dangling. Using a wing, she cut it toward me, slicing through the air. The tips of her wings were pointed and caught the light. Maybe they weren't metal, but they'd act like a weapon.

The tip of one just caught the front of my chest, ripping through my shirt but not cutting the skin. Even so, the heat off the point of her wing seared me, burning.

Wings were next to go then.

I crouched, leapt up and in the middle of my leap I shifted into my house cat form. Lilith screeched as she missed me. I went up and over her shoulder, twisting in mid-jump and shifting back to two legs. As I dropped, I grabbed the base of her wings, so I held her tight.

"I'll kill you! You're dead!" she screamed.

"Not likely you'll be the one to kill me. And it sure

as camel shit in the desert won't be today." I growled as I kicked her in the back, still holding her wings. Over and over I hit her, feeling things break, feeling her wings slowly tear from their connection to her body.

All the anger and frustration, all the holding back, all the keeping things in control went out the window. I was done with trusting anyone but Maks and Lila. I was done with this garbage. Lilith may be a demon, but I was a goddess-crowned alpha of the desert. A guardian. A Jinn. A shifter. These were my strengths, and even without my magic, that was enough. I was here to protect and save those I loved.

To keep the balance of our world.

I didn't realize I was screaming, didn't realize those screams were coming out of my actual mouth until I blinked and was looking up into Lila's terrified face.

I clamped my mouth shut and lifted a hand to her. "I'm okay."

"Are you sure because . . . that was . . . horrifying." She reached over and patted my cheek, and then I was sitting up, Maks was holding me and I was holding Lila.

But someone was missing.

I lifted a hand, remembering. "Fen. He got sucked through with Reyhan."

Lila burst into tears. "He tried to get that necklace off, but she was yanked through by the scorpion tail. He went with her."

"He will protect her." I nodded, thought it was a

shitty comfort. "Lila, we will go after them both. You know that."

"I do," she sobbed. "But it's just . . . this isn't how I thought it would end."

Me either.

Me fucking either.

nd of course, it wasn't the end of our day, not by a long shot. Maks helped me stand, and as we turned, the old woman stood blocking our way back into the castle. Not that I wanted to go through there, but with Fen gone we were trapped.

He'd done the right thing by going with Reyhan. He had. But we were screwed up shit creek without a paddle—or a dragon to carry us over it.

"You killed her." Arin looked past us, her face unreadable. "That . . . is unfortunate."

I braced myself, my hand going to the weapon that was Lilith. Her voice was silent as I gripped the handle of a sword. Not flail, not pole arm, but sword. This was her natural state then maybe?

Regardless.

"It was not how I saw things happening." My voice was scratchy from all the screaming.

Arin's eyes were hooded. "Nor was it how I saw it happening. I saw a dark-haired Jinn woman taking the army of rhuk and an army of unicorns to face Asag. I always thought it was my granddaughter." She squinted her eyes at me. "But you will do."

My eyebrows shot up. "Just like that, you'd trade her out?"

"She is dead. Asag is not. That must happen. So, I will help you. And like I said, my life was also in the balance. Dani would have killed me should I have failed her again." She bobbed her head once as if that was that.

"Yeah, I've had your help," Maks said. "It is not without its lies and costs."

"Everything costs." Arin smiled. "But that one beside you, I felt her battle a demon just now . . . and win. That is no small thing. She holds the source of magic *inside* of her without using it. That also is no small thing." She took a few steps toward me, her hands spread wide. "The trick with demons is to know their rules and use them against them. Are you ready to do that? Are you ready to use Asag's game against himself?"

"There is no other choice," I said. "We face Asag. As soon as the last challenge is completed."

Because I wasn't going to let a small thing like a footnote fuck me over. We would play by the rules and then we would use the rules to hang the demon up. I'd take this source of all magic to Pazuzu and be done with it.

Inside of me, Lilith rumbled that I was a fool for giving up all this potential power. I pushed my will against hers, shoving her away from the surface. I was not letting her out, not even a bit. For good measure I imagined a set of chains wrapped around each of her limbs, tying her down. She would not be getting free.

I rolled my wrist which rolled the sword in my hand. But before I could say anything else, someone pulled themselves up and over the edge of the roof. Late as always to the party.

"I am here, my love! To take you to the heights of pleasure with a flouncing that you will never forget!" Vahab flopped himself over the edge, soaking wet, disheveled. Right onto the chopped-up body of the Storm Queen. He grimaced and all but flew backward until he hit the far side of the wall, then glared at me. "Now you've doomed us all!"

"Lilith did it," I said, though I wasn't entirely unhappy. After all, I kind of wanted to chop Dani into pieces myself.

"But it is part of the game!" Vahab yelled. "The strongest two Jinn must flounce and create a child!"

I frowned. "That's stupid, all of it." What did Asag do? Just randomly try to come up with the hardest things to happen in order for him to get banished back to the realm of demons?

As soon as I thought it, I knew it. Yeah, that's exactly what he'd done. Fucker.

"That is not the exact wording," Arin said, her eyes drifting over Vahab. "It is the two *oldest* Jinn that must create a child. *Beyhron.* That is word for 'oldest,' and it is sometimes used for 'most powerful' in the demon tongue. In other words, it is often translated incorrectly."

Maks stared at her, his body tensing. "Then why the hell did you let Dani try to fuck me?"

"Because I could not convince her otherwise." Arin was terribly calm, as though it did not sting her that granddaughter had been killed. "Would you want to believe that your grandmother was the answer to a riddle you believed to be about you?"

I put my hands to my head. "So, you can have Vahab then, he is the oldest male Jinn."

Vahab squeaked. "What? No."

"He is the first Jinn," Lila piped up. "The very first. The one they stuck in the Vessel."

Arin's eyes lit up. "You are *that* Vahab?"

He closed his eyes and the life seemed to slip out of him. "I am."

I didn't feel bad. Vahab hadn't even asked about Fen. Maybe he—Vahab—was all about getting rid of Asag, but Fen had been his friend. Or I'd thought they'd been friends. And Vahab hadn't even tried to help him or stay with him as he'd died.

Arin crooked her finger at Vahab. He slowly got to

his feet and followed her out of the space, head down, his body obviously not interested in the old woman, not one bit.

"What if I cannot perform?" he muttered.

"She has something to help you," Maks called after Vahab. "These tiny blue pills."

Lila clung to me hard and the three of us stood there with the snap of the wind around us tugging at wings and hair alike. The silence was hard. Reyhan and Fen were gone. Taken. But I had to believe we would get them both back.

"What do we do now?"

"We look at all the rules that we have to follow, and we answer each quest that is demanded of us." I reached for Maks, and he took my hand, drawing me to him. Into the safety of his arms once more, I knew it wouldn't last. But like all things in my life, I took the quiet moments when I could. "We'll go after Reyhan and Fen. He'll protect her."

"I know he will," Lila whispered, "I know it."

And because I trusted Lila, I trusted Fen. I tightened my hold on Maks and leaned into him.

"We have to get this to Pazuzu." By this I meant the magic inside of me.

The wind around us picked up and the beat of massive wings filled the air. We turned to see a rhuk swooping toward us.

Cassandra let out a screeching call and landed precariously on the edge of the roof. She looked down at the broken body of Dani. Her head shot forward, and she plucked the Storm Queen up in pieces, flinging her arms, legs, torso and head into the sky. One by one each piece of her was caught by a rhuk and swallowed down.

"You freed my family." Cassandra tipped her head to us. "And so, we will go with you to face Asag."

She tipped her body to the side and a figure slid off her back, down her wings.

Pazuzu stood in front of us, dressed in blue just like before. "You have the source of all magic? Cassandra called to me when she felt Dani die."

I nodded, not sure I wanted to give it to him. "I do."

He smiled and tears gathered in his eyes. "It is a living thing. Do you understand?"

Again, I nodded, feeling the beat of it in my chest, like a second heart. "I know."

"Then set it free, desert guardian."

His words unleashed something in my body, and I started to shiver as the water I'd breathed in came back out, climbing up through my guts and up my throat to my mouth.

Yup, I puked out the source of all magic. Go me.

Glittering silver flecks and rainbows danced within it as it floated at head level, writhed once and then exploded.

Tiny droplets went everywhere, brushing against our faces, shooting out into the world at a speed that I could not follow with my eyes, but I could feel still.

Because one tiny droplet stayed with me.

Happy to be with me, happy to be a part of me.

Maks hung onto me, and I realized then that my legs had gone wobbly. "Thanks."

"I got you," he whispered.

Pazuzu bowed at the waist. "You have one more challenge, Zamira Reckless Wilson. One more challenge to see this through and face Asag."

I stared at him. "Let's hear it."

But before he could speak, a tug on the connections to my pride came through. As if . . . as if my brother and those I loved were far closer than they should have been.

I ran—okay, more like stumbled—to the side of the roof that looked toward the land. "Can you see them? Maks, Lila, do you feel that?"

"I do," Lila whispered. "I can feel them all!"

Cassandra flicked her beak. "Come, I will take you."

I climbed up on her back, and Maks followed. Lila clung to me as we rose in the air and swept away from the rooftop.

"I can feel them too," Maks said. "But how could they have come so far, so fast?"

I had a feeling I knew. And I was both grateful and horrified.

An army of unicorns would do it. Just as Arin had said she'd seen in her visions.

The rhuk dove down to the sands of the desert and I slid off her back. I could see them coming now, even through the dust storm that the herd had billowing around it.

In the lead was Bryce and Kiara riding Balder and the black mare.

The entire unicorn herd had come from Mamitu's stronghold, and they'd brought my pride with them.

Maks held up a fist and gave a greeting roar that I'd never heard from him, the sound sending shivers up and down my spine and giving me the urge to join him. Ah, fuck it.

I lifted a fist and let out my own roar, the sound of a jungle cat erupting out of me.

Bryce answered us with a roar of his own, one that drove away some of my fears, one that echoed across the sand. The bellow of a male lion come to protect his family. To protect me. My family was here, and it took all I had not to have a little breakdown. Because it was one thing to know your family loved you, but another entirely when they showed up in the hardest points of your life.

"We can do this," Lila said. "Then imitate the action of the lion; stiffen the sinews, summon up the blood." She bumped her head against mine.

Lila was abso-fucking-lutely right. We would face Asag together.

And then he would see what it meant to take on the guardians of the desert.

NEXT UP!

And if you can't wait to read something, try the gem on the next page on for size with over 2500 reviews so far!

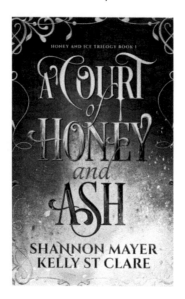

Orphaned. Trained to fight. Raised to fear the power of Underhill. Secretly in love with a man who doesn't want me.

"Get ready for a wild ride! Nothing less than I'd expect from these two authors!"

ABOUT THE AUTHOR

Check out the links below. Or not, I'm honestly so sleep deprived I'm struggling to remember my own name, never mind where the hell you can find me online.

Seriously, who thought a puppy was a good idea? I think this is worse than a baby! #monster #babyvelociraptor #BabyLila